BAD

NICOLA MARSH

Copyright © Nicola Marsh 2015
Published by Nicola Marsh 2015

All the characters in this book have no existence outside the imagination of the author and have no relation whatsoever to anyone bearing the same name or names. They're not distantly inspired by any individual known or unknown to the author and all the incidents in the book are pure invention.

All rights reserved including the right of reproduction in any form. The text or any part of the publication may not be reproduced or transmitted in any form without the written permission of the publisher.

The author acknowledges the copyrighted or trademarked status and trademark owners of the word marks mentioned in this work of fiction.

Wyatt Harrison is a geek and proud of it.
The IT freelancer prefers delving into the mysteries of motherboards than women. Until he upgrades the computer system at Vegas's premier dance venue Burlesque Bombshells, where he's confronted by the biggest mystery of them all, stunning choreographer Ashlin O'Meara.

Ashlin prefers brawn to brains. She likes her men uncomplicated for a reason. But there's something about Wyatt that she can't resist.
Unable to achieve satisfaction in the bedroom for years, he could be the guy to push all her right buttons.

However, Wyatt's no fool, and in agreeing to a short-term fling with the sexy geek, will her devastating secret be revealed, resulting in the collapse of her carefully constructed life?

ONE

Wyatt Harrison took one step into the room filled with beautiful people and wished he hadn't come.

This so wasn't his scene.

Upgrading IT systems at Burlesque Bombshells he could handle. Socializing with the gorgeous women who worked at the establishment, not so much.

Though tonight wasn't about mingling with the dancers he wouldn't see again after this freelance contract finished.

The only reason he'd shown up at this cocktail party was to meet Steele Harrison, his half-brother.

Zane, the other Aussie half-sibling he'd known nothing about until a month ago, had said Steele would be here. So Wyatt had knocked back a few tequila shots to quell his anti-party phobia and rocked up.

But he'd barely entered and spotted Zane when a woman bore down on him.

Not just any woman. Ashlin O'Meara. Lead choreographer at Burlesque Bombshells. She'd haunted his dreams for weeks. His secret fantasy. Tall. Lithe. Long red hair. Big blue eyes. Full lips that made him hard just thinking about what they could do. And a soft lilting Irish accent that was sexy as hell.

They'd met briefly while he'd been working in the CEO's office last week. That encounter had been memorable for the simple fact he hadn't been able to string a few words together before bolting. She'd probably been laughing about his gaucheness ever since, while he couldn't forget the soft skin of her palm as it had lingered in his during their introductory handshake.

"Glad you could make it," she said, her beauty even more astounding close up. "I was hoping you'd be here."

"Why?" he blurted, his characteristic social awkwardness making him wish he could turn and run.

He didn't understand females, not like metadata and motherboards. Women made him uneasy, a complex puzzle he had no hope of solving.

Ashlin smiled and leaned in close. Close enough he could smell a seductive spicy fragrance that addled him as much as her nearness. "Because after that first time we met in Chantal's office, I've wanted to get to know you better."

Wyatt stared at her like she'd lost her mind. Women didn't come onto him. The only hook-ups he'd had were at IT conventions, with fellow female geeks who didn't flirt. Women willing to come up to his room after a few drinks and a less than scintillating conversation that focused solely on computers. It suited him, the lack of emotional connection.

Which begged the question, why was this striking woman coming onto him? Not that he didn't like it. Hell, his gonads liked it just fine. But her proximity unnerved him. *She* unnerved him. And he felt inept enough in social situations without adding her to the mix.

"You want to get to know me better?" He sounded

incredulous, like she'd asked him to strip naked on the spot. "Trust me, there's not much to tell."

"I beg to differ." She touched his arm and Wyatt could've sworn he'd misconnected wires; the jolt was that powerful. Swift and sizzling and strong enough to fry his brain. "You're an intelligent guy. I'm sure we could talk for hours."

If he had Ashlin alone for hours, talk would be the furthest thing from his mind.

He shook his head, trying to clear it. Didn't help. "You're into geeks?" As if.

"Maybe I'm into you," she said, her fingertips gliding down his forearm, slow and sensual, stopping to tease his wrist with a tickle before she stepped back and shrugged, drawing his attention to her shoulders, where the strap of a shimmery tank top seemed in grave danger of slipping off. "And I'd like to pick your brain about a computer problem."

Disconcerted by the urge to snag that damn strap and tug it all the way down, he glowered, hoping she'd get the message to leave him alone. "I don't talk business after hours."

Her lips curved into a coy smile that had him staring longer than polite. "Can't you make an exception this one time?"

"No," he said, tearing his gaze away from her luscious mouth to search the room for Zane again.

He needed an exit strategy. Pronto.

"You're not very sociable." She tilted her head, studying him. "Or is it just me that makes you uncomfortable?"

He bit back 'it's you'.

"Parties aren't my thing," he said, spotting Zane, who had his back turned and was deep in conversation with a guy. Hopefully it was Steele, giving him the perfect out. "If you'll excuse me, I need to meet someone—"

"Wait." She laid a hand on his arm and damned if his skin didn't prickle again. "Can we grab a coffee sometime?"

The hint of vulnerability in her eyes startled him. "Why?"

"Isn't it obvious?" She blinked, her bold blue gaze challenging him, and he wondered if he'd imagined the vulnerability a second ago.

Obvious? Not to him. She'd have to hit him over the head with a sledgehammer for him to process that a woman as hot as her could be interested in a geek like him.

"Enlighten me."

Her fingers squeezed his forearm gently. "You're interesting and different—"

"Thanks, maybe some other time."

Before he could second-guess his dumbass decision to dump the stunning redhead, who for some unfathomable reason wanted to get to know him, he managed a terse nod and eased his arm out of her grasp.

The faster he made a beeline for Zane, the better.

ASHLIN STARED AT WYATT, practically running through the crowd to get away from her, and grinned.

Wasn't every day a guy tried to break the minute mile to escape her. Ratcheted up her curiosity about him even more.

"Leave the poor guy alone." Chantal Kramer, her boss and friend, elbowed her in the ribs. "You're scaring him."

"He's adorable," Ashlin said.

Chantal's eyebrow rose. "And not your type, so what gives?"

Ashlin knew exactly why she'd targeted Wyatt but no way in hell would she tell Chantal. Her friend had an uncanny knack for seeing right through her and if Chantal guessed the truth...no one in her new life knew about her past and she had to keep it that way.

Ashlin feigned a laugh. "I have a type?"

"Hell yeah." Chantal flexed a bicep and struck a bodybuilder's pose. "You usually go for the brawny, brainless types."

Again, Ashlin had her reasons. Reasons she'd be keeping to herself. "Perhaps I need a change of scenery?"

"But Wyatt?" Chantal lowered her arms and beckoned her into a corner, away from the partygoers. "He's a good guy, Ash. And he's doing an amazing job updating my IT system." Chantal jabbed her in the arm. "Not to mention he's Zane's half-brother and the love of my life will kill me if you do anything to scare Wyatt off considering they're putting in some serious bonding time after meeting recently."

"Love of my life? Listen to you." Ashlin pretended to stick two fingers down her throat and gag. "What happened to the confident, ballsy businesswoman who didn't have time to date because running Burlesque Bombshells was her life?"

"Zane happened." Chantal sighed, her gaze drifting toward her Australian boyfriend on the opposite side of the room. "And I still can't believe it, to be honest."

Zane glanced up at that moment and locked gazes with Chantal. Ashlin could've sworn electricity arced overhead between them.

"Believe it. The guy's smitten." Ashlin hadn't meant to sound bitter. She was truly happy that her workaholic friend had found love. But her inner cynic couldn't be ignored. She'd thought she'd found love once. It had turned to shit. Along with her life as a result of the fallout.

"The feeling's mutual," Chantal said, a blush reddening her cheeks. "Which is why you can't toy with Wyatt."

"Who says I'm toying?"

Chantal rolled her eyes. "Please. I haven't seen you in a relationship since you started working for me years ago. You date. Briefly. Then move on. That's if you date at all."

"I've been in a deliberate drought." Ashlin shot Chantal a pointed look. "Same as you, pre-hot-Aussie-footballer, remember?"

Chantal tapped her bottom lip. "I had my reasons. What's yours?"

What could Ashlin say? That she'd rather relax at home after work than make meaningless small talk with a guy she wouldn't see more than once or twice? That dating himbos was easier because they didn't demand anything beyond a brief physical interlude? That investing in any guy for longer than two seconds equaled a guaranteed broken heart?

She could've said all those things. Instead, she settled for, "I don't have time for a relationship."

Chantal cupped her hands around her mouth, as if magnifying whatever she was going to say. "BS alert."

"Ssh." Ashlin laughed and swatted her friend's hands. "When you introduced me to Wyatt in your office last week, I felt like we clicked."

Chantal puffed out her cheeks then exhaled. "You did. Miranda and I both saw the sparks. Seemed like you two were alone in the room."

Ashlin had felt it too, which is why she'd deliberately approached Wyatt tonight. She didn't trust *sparks*. Not anymore. So she'd figured if she tried her usual brash approach on the guy, it would get it out of her system.

Sadly, talking to Wyatt, seeing how recalcitrant he was, piqued her interest. She may not be interested in anything beyond a fling but there was something about the surly guy that had her wanting to know more.

"Maybe you could get the lowdown on him from Zane?"

"No way." Chantal held up her hands and backed away a little. "I'm not getting involved in this...whatever it is you're doing."

"It's called dating." Ashlin gestured at Zane. "You know, that thing you're doing with Lover Boy over there."

Chantal's eyes widened. "You actually want to date Wyatt?"

"Maybe...no...hell, damned if I know."

But Ashlin did know. She didn't want to date Wyatt. She wanted a little one-on-one time so she could discover why he had her on edge.

Guys never made an impression on her and certainly not beyond a week. The fact she'd cornered him tonight because she hadn't been able to stop thinking about him since they'd met meant something. And the fully intended to find out what that *something* was.

"Just go easy on the guy, that's all I'm saying, okay?" Chantal leaned in to kiss her on the cheek. "You could do with a little romance, Ash, but don't go hurting my boyfriend's brother."

"Like I would."

Besides, she'd have to be emotionally invested to hurt Wyatt or be hurt herself, and she had no intention of getting that close.

To any guy.

Ever again.

TWO

As Wyatt approached Zane, his half-brother's goofy grin grew.

"What are you smirking at?" Wyatt scowled, not in the mood for any shit, courtesy of Ashlin bamboozling him to the point he couldn't think straight.

"You." Zane slugged him on the arm. "Very entertaining, watching you crash and burn with Ashlin."

"By choice, smartass."

Zane's eyebrows rose. "You knocked her back?"

"She's not my type." Wyatt expected a lightning bolt to strike him down any second for that monumental lie.

Zane guffawed as he jostled him. "So you're a fibber as well as an idiot."

"Quit it."

Wyatt didn't need Zane reiterating what he already knew: he was a dumbass for not taking Ashlin up on her offer or at the very least, reciprocating her interest.

Zane's grin faded, his expression turning somber, but he couldn't hide the mischief in his eyes. "You know dancers are extremely flexible, right? So it's probably a good thing you didn't hook up, what with you being a computer geek, you could've done yourself an injury—"

"Shut up," Wyatt said, joining in Zane's chuckles. "Is Steele here?"

Thankfully, Zane bought his change of subject. "Yeah, entered not long after you did, got waylaid by the yoga instructor."

"You Aussie Harrisons don't waste any time, do you?"

Zane squared his shoulders. "I'll have you know it took me a good month to get Chantal to realize she couldn't resist me."

"For a CEO of her own company, hooking up with you is a dumb move."

Zane's perpetual grin broadened. "Don't forget I'm bigger than you, squirt. I can take you."

Before Wyatt could respond, a guy behind him spoke. "He's been trying that line on me for years. Bullshit trying to baffle brains as usual."

The guy stepped into view and held out his hand. "Steele Harrison."

Wyatt struggled to hide his surprise. His other half-brother was a blonder, blue-eyed version of himself. Six foot. Lean. Wiry. With a vague hint of a frown line between his brows.

"Wyatt. Pleased to meet you." He shook his half-brother's hand, not surprised Steele tried to squeeze his down to the bones.

Zane had clued him in that Steele was a control freak and had to be in charge of every situation, from the boardroom to a party. Guess that's where their similarities ended. Wyatt preferred blending into a crowd any day.

"We look alike." Steele studied Wyatt's face, as if

looking for clues to a mystery he wasn't sure he wanted to solve.

"Yeah, could be worse." Wyatt jerked a thumb at Zane. "We could look like him."

Steele let out a bark of laughter. "I reckon we're going to be mates."

"Yeah, brains trump brawn any day," Wyatt drawled, secretly thrilled to be swapping banter with his half-brothers.

He'd never been close to Kurt, his football star brother, for the simple fact they had little in common. Plus he wouldn't be human if he didn't resent Kurt for their father's obvious favoritism.

Christopher Harrison, the doyen of sporting goods in America, valued strength and courage on a football field. He didn't think much of talent in the IT arena.

"If you two are going to gang up on me five seconds after meeting for the first frigging time, I'm outta here," Zane said, an obvious bluff, considering he looked immensely pleased Steele had accepted him so easily.

"He won't leave," Steele said. "Chantal has his balls in her back pocket."

Wyatt laughed. Thank god Steele had the same dry sense of humor as his Aussie brother.

"You two losers are jealous." Zane snapped his fingers. "Hey, speaking of hot women, what's going on with you and Miranda? I saw her bail you up at the door."

"That yoga chick is crazy." Steele made loopy circles at his temple. "She deliberately trod on my toes in the corridor before we entered and then she went ballistic."

Zane's eyes narrowed. "What aren't you telling us?"

"Nothing." Steele's expression, a mix of guilt and angelic, made Wyatt snicker.

Since he'd been working here the last few weeks, he'd gotten to observe most of the girls firsthand. People didn't notice him because he worked in the background. He liked it that way. It enabled him to make people-reading an art form.

Pity he couldn't get an accurate read on Ashlin.

From what he'd seen, Chantal, Ashlin and Miranda were tight. Where Chantal and Ashlin were tall, lithe, blonde and redhead respectively, Miranda was a petite brunette who looked capable of packing a punch. Whatever Steele had done, he would've paid money to see her take him down.

"So Zane tells me you're updating the IT systems here?" Steele said.

Wyatt nodded, admiring Steele's change of topic, something he'd used to great effect earlier. "Yeah. Some of the stuff is pretty archaic so it's an upgrade."

"We should talk shop one day," Steele said.

Wyatt would like nothing better. "You run your own digital marketing company?"

"Uh-huh. Promote businesses worldwide."

Zane snorted. "He's underselling as usual. Think of every major brand and he's probably marketing it online."

"Impressive," Wyatt said, his admiration increasing because of Steele's modesty. Some of the guys he knew in IT would spend endless hours boasting about their success. He preferred the quiet achievers.

"No idea why you're blowing smoke up my arse, Zane, but quit it." Steele leaned over to Wyatt and jerked a thumb at Zane. "He's the superstar in the family and thinks I have a hang-up because of it."

"Know the feeling."

Steele nodded. "So Kurt's a big deal in football, I hear?"

"A superstar ten times over." Wyatt kept the bitterness from his tone, but he must've let slip a tell because his half-brothers eyed him with speculation.

"Bet that comes at a price," Zane said. "I should know."

"Yeah, must be tough beating models and actresses off with a stick," Steele said, with what Wyatt was fast recognizing as his signature dry humor.

Zane rolled his eyes. "I'll leave you nerds together while I go hang out with my gorgeous girlfriend."

Steele pressed a thumb to his forehead. "Yep, under this, and balls in her pocket."

"Fuck off," Zane said, without a hint of malice. "Catch you later."

As Zane wandered off in search of Chantal, Steele turned back to him. "Is the redhead your girlfriend?"

Wyatt liked Steele's bluntness but talking women with a guy he'd just met, albeit his half-brother, felt plain weird. "Nah, she's a choreographer here."

"You seemed pretty tight?"

"She asked me out," he blurted, sounding like an idiot. He never shared personal stuff with anyone but Steele was different. He sensed a kindred spirit, a guy who'd prefer getting lost in his work than socializing. Then again, he knew next to nothing about the guy so maybe he was off base.

"And that's a bad thing because?"

Wyatt shrugged. "Not sure what her angle is."

Steele frowned. "She has an angle?"

"Girls who look like her don't usually go for guys like me."

Steele's mouth quirked into a wry smile. "Considering we look alike, I beg to differ."

Wyatt chuckled. "So you pull a lot of babes in Oz, huh?"

"I do okay."

By the way Steele straightened his shoulders and puffed his chest out, Wyatt reckoned he did better than okay.

"Steady girlfriend?"

Steele shook his head. "No one special. You?"

"Same."

Truth was Wyatt had never had a girlfriend. The occasional fling at conferences was so far from a relationship it wasn't funny. He preferred it that way. But watching Zane with Chantal, he had to admit to a twinge of jealousy.

Steele beckoned to some barstools nearby and they sat. "So you don't know her that well?"

"Not really. We met in the office once and then she waylays me the second I walked in here."

"Maybe it's the Harrison charm?"

Wyatt snorted. "My charm works fine on software. Elsewhere? Not so much."

"What about your brother?"

Wyatt bit back his first retort, 'don't you mean *our* brother'. Zane had clued him in that Steele visiting the States was a big deal, that he was willing to meet his half-brothers but didn't want Christopher mentioned, that he was wary of his US family in general.

"Kurt has more women than he knows what to do with."

"Lucky bastard." Funnily enough, Steele made him sound far from lucky with the right amount of derision. "Do you guys hang out much?"

"Rarely. But he'll want to meet you."

"Yeah?" Steele looked pleased for a moment before he schooled his expression into an inscrutable mask that Wyatt guessed was his version of a poker face.

"He likes to suss out the competition."

"Competition?" The furrow between Steele's brows

deepened. "I don't get it."

"Christopher's company is worth millions. Kurt thought he was the eldest so he'd inherit. Then you come along."

"I don't want that bastard's money." Steele scowled, his eyes flashing fire.

"Ditto, but Kurt doesn't know that, and considering you're the eldest Harrison, he'll be nervous."

Steele cocked his head. "You call him Christopher?"

"We've never been close."

Understatement of the year. Thinking about his father made Wyatt want to rub his chest to ease the ache that flared with anything remotely connected to dear old Dad.

"At least he was around," Steele said, resentment twisting his mouth.

Wyatt understood Steele's bitterness all too well. Christopher may have abandoned his Australian sons to start a new family in the States, but their father had never been around for him either. Not in any real way that mattered.

"Physically, maybe, but that's where it ended." Wyatt shrugged like it meant little when in fact he despised his father for how callous he could be.

Steele opened his mouth, as if he wanted to say more, then closed it again, his lips compressed into a thin, angry line.

Wyatt felt obliged to fill the silence. "You know he'll want to meet you too."

"Tough," Steele said, anger evident in his rigid neck muscles. "I don't give a flying fuck what the old man wants."

"My sentiments exactly, but a word of advice?"

When Steele remained silent, Wyatt continued. "Christopher will never change. He's a selfish, narcissistic bastard and even the ever-optimistic Zane realized it damn quick. But you don't want to head home filled with regret and that's what'll probably happen."

"What do you know about regret?" Steele snarled, before tempering it with a tap on the shoulder in silent apology.

"I know enough." Sometimes, it felt like regret had become Wyatt's middle name.

He regretted not bonding with his family as a kid. He regretted not following his dream of being a game app designer. Most of all, he regretted shutting himself away as a teen, losing himself in a virtual world to the point he had no idea how to interact with women in the real world.

Women like Ashlin.

"Sorry, mate." Steele slapped him on the back. "As you can see, Christopher's a sore topic for me."

"Don't blame you," Wyatt said. "The way he left you and Zane in Australia to start a new life over here and never got in contact again? Unbe-fucking-lievable."

"You got that right."

Wyatt glimpsed pain—the type of soul-deep pain that makes your bones ache—in Steele's eyes.

"But let's not waste another second talking about him." Some of the tension drained from Steele's face. "What are you going to do about the redhead?"

What Wyatt wanted to do with Ashlin couldn't be articulated in public.

"Nothing."

Steele's eyes narrowed, as if he was thinking hard. "Why don't you call her bluff?"

"How?"

Steele sniggered. "Sometimes beautiful women who are super confident enjoy toying with shy guys. It's a game to them. Maybe you should call her on it?"

"I don't think Ashlin's like that—"

"How well do you know her?"

"I don't."

"Then how do you know she's not playing you?"

Wyatt didn't have a frigging clue why Ashlin had asked him out but if what Steele said was true, he'd be pissed.

Was she toying with him because she could? Expecting him to run because he had 'social outcast' or 'computer geek' tattooed on his forehead?

"Do women really do that kind of thing?"

Steele chuckled. "Mate, women who look like that stunning redhead are capable of anything."

The more he thought about Ashlin goading him for her own amusement, the angrier Wyatt got. Who the hell did she think she was?

"Call her bluff, huh?"

Steele nodded. "Yep. You be the aggressor. Take her up on her offer. Push the envelope. See how she reacts."

Steele's plan sounded good. Except Wyatt wouldn't have a clue how to push Ashlin to do anything.

"Think about it," Steele said. "I'm outta here, but maybe we can meet up for a drink tomorrow and you can tell me how you got on?"

"Sure." Wyatt shook his brother's hand. This time, Steele didn't try to fracture every bone. "That'd be great."

"See you then." Steele jerked a thumb over his shoulder, where Zane was cozying up with Chantal. "Say bye to the dickhead for me."

"Shall do."

"No worries." Steele paused. "With the redhead? Don't do anything I wouldn't do."

Wyatt's nervous chuckle belied his nerves.

Because what the hell would he do with Ashlin?

THREE

"See that guy who's leaving?" Miranda elbowed Ashlin in the ribs. "The one by the door?"

Ashlin craned her neck, catching a glimpse of dirty-blond hair and a designer suit. "Yeah, that's Zane's brother, Steele."

"*That's* Zane's brother?" Miranda's eyes widened. "Uh-oh."

"Why? What happened?"

Miranda gnawed on her bottom lip. "Uh...I may have called him an uptight prick."

Ashlin winced. "Ouch."

Miranda groaned. "How was I supposed to know the guy's practically Chantal's family?"

"Chantal and Zane aren't married," Ashlin said, knowing it was a matter of time, her friend was that smitten with the hot Aussie.

"But they will be." Miranda pointed at the far end of the bar. "Take a look. Have you ever seen anything so sickening in all your life?"

Ashlin glanced over in time to see Zane say something

very dirty if Chantal's shocked yet mischievous expression was any indication. Closely followed by a lip lock that would need a crowbar to pry them apart.

"They barely know each other." A fact that surprised Ashlin on a daily basis since the hunky Aussie had bowled into town.

In all the years she'd known Chantal, she'd never seen the bold blonde as anything other than a man-eater. A woman so confident she could make a guy wither with a single glance. Chantal rarely dated so the fact she'd fallen hard for the Aussie in a month made Ashlin wonder if she should buy ice skates for the newly frozen Hades.

"When you connect on that level, what's to know?" Miranda's wistful sigh drew Ashlin's attention away from the happy couple. "I'd love to find a guy who looks at me the way Zane looks at her."

Surprised by the sudden sadness down-turning her friend's mouth, Ashlin slipped her arm around Miranda's shoulders and hugged. "You will."

"I'm starting to seriously doubt it." Miranda rested her head on Ashlin's shoulder a moment before straightening. "Mamma's been planning a big Italian wedding for as long as I can remember and the fact I'm turning thirty soon means the pressure is sky-high."

"She wants grandkids, huh?"

Miranda screwed up her nose. "You'd think having my three older sisters produce ten kids between them would be enough?" She shook her head. "*Nooooo*...apparently I'm neglecting my duty as a good Italian girl to find a good husband, make a good home and produce a brood of good kids."

Ashlin laughed at Miranda's faux Italian accent. "Here's a tip for you, babe. Hanging around Chantal's cocktail parties won't help you find a guy, considering the dancers are all female."

Miranda's gaze drifted to the door again. "Steele Harrison looked the part but what a jerk."

"What happened?"

"He gave me crap about my necklace so I trod on his toes."

Ashlin glanced down at Miranda's signature stilettos. "With those?"

She had the grace to blush. "Yeah. Must've hurt."

"Remind me never to comment on your jewelry."

Miranda fingered the wooden beaded and feathered string hanging around her neck. "This stuff promotes my business so what would Mr. High-and-Mighty know about it?"

Ashlin tended to agree with Steele about the ugliness of Miranda's necklace but she would never tell her friend that. "What did he say?"

"Made some wisecrack about being allergic to birds so I shouldn't wear a menagerie around my neck." Miranda's quick look-away suggested there was more behind this story.

"Why would he have a dig at you for no reason?"

"Well..." Miranda's faux innocence wasn't convincing. "I may have bailed him up and said our cocktail parties are private, and not open to every sleazy troll who wanders back here from the showroom."

Ashlin let out a whoop of laughter. "You thought he was a peep from the audience?"

Miranda nodded. "Guess he didn't take too kindly to being mistaken for a patron." She chuckled. "Or being called a sleazy troll."

"And then you stomped on him and called him an uptight prick?" Ashlin couldn't contain her giggles. "Even though he's cute, perhaps you should set your sights elsewhere."

"I'm not setting my sights on anyone." Miranda folded her arms and pouted. "Besides, you looked cozy with Wyatt when my battle with Steele ended."

"He's nice enough." *And not interested in me, just the way I like it.*

"You know he's shy and you'll have to put the moves on him?"

Which is exactly why she'd done it. Knowing Wyatt wouldn't reciprocate meant she'd done her duty in the dating stakes for another few weeks. The part where she felt oddly rejected when he walked away? She hadn't counted on that.

"I tried."

Miranda wolf-whistled. "And? When are you two going out?"

"We're not."

"Why?"

"He said no."

Miranda's eyes widened. "To you? The guy must be blind or gay."

Ashlin suspected neither and she wasn't going to waste another moment mulling why Wyatt didn't want to have a coffee with her.

"Not to worry." Ashlin winked. "His loss."

"You said it, girlfriend." Miranda's smile faded. "You know we're a couple of pathetic losers, right, rocking up to this party every four weeks for the last few years without a hot guy in tow?"

Ashlin grabbed two shot glasses from a passing waiter and handed one to Miranda. "Who needs a guy when we've got tequila?"

"True." Miranda tapped her glass lightly against Ashlin's. "Drink up."

However, as Ashlin tossed back the liquor and it burned a path down her throat, she couldn't help but wonder why Wyatt had said no.

FOUR

Wyatt knew he was a sad case.

Leaving a cocktail party brimming with hot babes to check on a systems update would get him committed by any self-respecting guy. But that's the way he rolled. He could understand IT configurations. Women, not so much.

As he let himself into Chantal's office where he stored his equipment for this job, he pondered Steele's advice. While the brother he'd just met could be talking out his ass, it made him madder than hell to think Ashlin had targeted him for kicks.

"Fuck," he muttered, scanning a mini hard-drive to detect any faults, wishing he knew enough about women to figure out what her motivation had been.

Not that it mattered. He'd be winding up this job shortly and the chances of running into her again were minimal. Suited him just fine.

Then why the twinge of regret that he hadn't taken her up on her offer?

Hell, she hadn't invited him back to her place for the night. She'd suggested coffee. Could barely be labeled a frigging date. Yet he'd baulked anyway. It sucked having his entire world revolve around computers so the infrequent hook-ups he'd had were with gamer girls.

When a woman like Ashlin spoke to him, he could barely respond, not without sounding a dufus.

The door to the office swung open. Great, that's all he needed, for Chantal to bust him hiding out here rather than socializing at her party. She'd insisted he attend and when Zane had got on his case too, he hadn't come up with a plausible excuse fast enough.

Eager to escape, he powered down the hard-drive and slipped it into his pocket, in time to see Ashlin enter the office and shut the door. His heart stalled as he watched her bend over the desk, black skintight denim outlining a sensational ass and long legs that promised heaven. She rummaged through the mess, searching for something, oblivious to his ogling. Guess that answered his first question, that she'd followed him.

He should slip out undetected but as he edged toward the door, he found himself hesitating when she slammed her hand on the desk.

"Dammit," she muttered, running a hand through her hair, a deep russet with shimmery copper threads that captured the light as she moved. Yeah, he was that much of a dumbass with her he was analyzing the color of her hair.

"Need some help?"

She jumped and whirled around, her hand pressed to her chest. "You scared the crap out of me."

"Sorry," he said, not apologetic in the slightest, glad he wasn't the only one off-kilter for once. "I'm in here for work. What's your excuse?"

She tilted her nose up, as if he didn't deserve to know.

"Chantal can't find her phone. We tried ringing it but it's off so she sent out a search party."

"I'm assuming she hasn't got that *find a phone* app running."

She glared at him. "Guess you assumed right, Einstein."

To his surprise, he found himself grinning. "That's the best you can come up with? Einstein?"

Her eyes narrowed to fiery blue slits. "Would you prefer asshole?"

This time, he laughed outright. "Wow, you're shitty when a guy turns you down."

"Your loss." She shrugged and gave her hair another toss over her shoulder for good measure.

"Or yours." He strode toward her, buoyed by the flicker of alarm in her eyes.

Goddamn, Steele had been right. She'd picked him because she hadn't expected him to accept her invitation. She'd been toying with him. But rather than the earlier anger flooding him, he was curious. Why would a stunner, who could have any guy she wanted, target him, an insecure guy who would probably refuse her?

Intrigued against his better judgment, he stopped two feet away, close enough to smell the same exotic fragrance that had muddled his senses earlier. "Maybe I've changed my mind."

"About?"

"Taking you up on that offer of coffee."

"Too bad I've changed my mind." Her wide-eyed gaze dropped to his lips, as she licked hers.

"Yeah, too bad." He took a step closer, bringing her within touching distance.

Barely an inch separated them and he heard her sharp

intake of breath, felt the heat radiating off her bare skin exposed by the scrap of silk masquerading as a top.

"Why did you ask me out?" He reached out, trailed a fingertip down her arm, skating over a smattering of goosebumps.

"Because you seem like a nice guy." Her voice hitched as he grazed her wrist, her palm.

"And because you thought I'd say no."

Awareness flared in her eyes. "That's BS."

"Is it?" His hand rested on her hip. Slid slowly around to the small of her back. "You thought the geek would be intimidated by your beauty."

A small smile curved her lips. "You think I'm beautiful?"

"Do you seriously need the validation?" Even now, she was playing him, fishing for compliments and Wyatt had had enough.

Time to call her bluff.

"I need..." She sighed and lowered her gaze.

"What?"

He wanted her to say 'you' but that was wishful thinking. Strong, independent women didn't need anything or anybody, least of all a guy so far out of his depth he needed a lifebuoy ASAP.

"What do you need?"

She raised her eyes to meet his again, and the uncertainty he glimpsed floored him.

"I don't know."

Her vulnerability scared him more than her overt come-on earlier, and before he could second-guess his impulse, he blurted, "I think you need this," and kissed her.

She gasped in surprise, giving him access to her lush mouth and he didn't need a second invitation, his tongue taunting hers. Teasing. Challenging.

She moaned and he angled his head, deepening the kiss to the point where he could barely breathe. He didn't care. He'd happily pass out from lack of oxygen if he could devour her for longer than a minute.

God, had he ever kissed like this? Deep. Long. Hot. Moist kisses that never ended. He reached for her, his hands sliding from her waist to her ribcage to her boobs.

She wrenched her mouth from his, staring at him as if he'd lost his mind. Which he had, around the time they'd first played tonsil hockey moments ago.

"What the hell was that?" Her chest heaved, her blue eyes flashing with...fear?

Fuck, was she scared of him? He may not be good at flirting with women but usually when he kissed them they enjoyed it as much as he did.

"That was me showing you I'm not some idiot you can jerk around."

Anger replaced the fear as her eyes narrowed. "You were trying to prove a point?"

"Yeah, I don't like being played for a fool."

Her shoulders sagged a little as a wistful sigh barely above a whisper escaped her lips. "I don't think you're a fool."

"Then prove it." He stepped back, needing to put some space between them before he was tempted to reach for her again. "Tell me why you asked me out."

She glanced away and huffed out a long breath. "Honestly?"

He waited, intrigued by what she'd say.

"You seemed a safe bet," she said, a faint blush tingeing her cheeks. "A guy who wouldn't put the moves on me."

"But why single me out in the first place? Why ask me out?"

Didn't make sense. If she didn't want a guy to put the moves on her—like he'd just done with that kiss—she could've avoided guys altogether at the party.

"You ask a lot of questions." She pouted and damned if it didn't make him want to kiss her again.

"And you aren't giving me any answers that make sense."

She cocked a hip, switching from embarrassed to teasing, leaving him more confused. "So? What are you going to do about it?"

Turned on by her sass, he touched her cheek. "Are you angling for another lip lock, taunting me?"

"You wish."

"Honey, you have no idea how much."

Her eyes darkened to indigo and the tip of her tongue flickered out to moisten her bottom lip. "Look, this has been nice and all, but I need to get back to the party—"

"No you don't. We're going to have that coffee. Now."

The corners of her mouth twitched. "Already told you, I reneged on the offer."

"Too bad, because I have a top line coffee machine in my hotel suite." He threw it out there, the ultimate challenge, knowing she wouldn't accept.

He'd called her bluff, as Steele had advised, but rather than feeling vindicated, he felt like an idiot.

Because he'd give anything for her to take him up on his offer.

She chuckled. Not the reaction he'd expected. "You're trying to outplay the player?"

He schooled his face into nonchalance. "Don't know what you're talking about."

"Sure you do." This time, she advanced on him. So close. Not close enough. "Okay, let's do this."

His neurons, usually firing at an accelerated rate, failed to compute her implication. Or perhaps that kiss had short-circuited his brain completely. "Do what?"

"Go have that coffee in your suite." Her mischievous smile made him want to kiss her again. "You up for it?"

Struggling to hide his shock, he nodded. "Sure, let's go."

"I'll need to let Chantal know I didn't find her phone—"

"She'll figure it out." Besides, he had the damndest urge to grab her hand and make a run for his suite before she changed her mind.

"You in a hurry to ply me with caffeine?"

He liked her teasing, liked her with a cocky smile rather than the fear he'd glimpsed earlier.

"Sweetheart, this is going to be the best damn coffee you've ever had."

He held out his hand, even now expecting her to bolt.

Instead, she placed her hand in his. "Then what are we waiting for?"

FIVE

Ashlin had known entering Wyatt's hotel suite was a bad idea. A monumentally stupid idea. But she'd never been able to back down from a challenge and having him see right through her, then goad her about it...No, she *had* to be here on principle.

Nice in theory, but now that she struggled not to pace his luxurious suite, the practice was a hell of a lot harder.

"Drink?" He held up a tiny bottle of vodka in one hand, whiskey in the other. "Or there's plenty more options in the minibar."

Hell, alcohol was the last thing she needed; he had her in enough of a spin.

"I thought you said coffee was on offer?"

"Oh." The corners of his mouth twitched. "So you really want coffee?"

"That's what I'm here for." She perched on the back of a chair. "One coffee, then I'm out of here."

"That's what they all say." He smiled, and it transformed his face from serious to heart-stoppingly handsome. "But then they get a glimpse of this" —he gestured at himself— "and they can't help but stay." He paused for dramatic effect. "After they've torn off my clothes, of course."

"Of course," she said, unable to resist grinning back at him. "But I'm strong-willed. I'll try to resist."

She thought she heard him murmur, "Please don't," as he padded barefoot into the bathroom to fill the kettle. She'd never found feet sexy before, but there was something about Wyatt's long tanned feet, perfect arch and neat toes that had her staring and imagining what they'd feel like rubbing against her calves as their legs entwined in bed...

"Cream and sugar?"

"Cream, no sugar," she said, mentally cursing herself for not making a run for it while he'd been in the bathroom.

Pigheadedness demanded she never back down from a challenge, then there was the kind of stubbornness that landed her in places she'd rather not be.

Like when she first ran away from her home in Ireland and ended up in a squalid Dublin bedsit. Or the time she'd slept on a park bench in London. Or the most destructive time, when she'd sabotaged a relationship by ending up in a clinic that effectively destroyed her dancing career before it had begun.

So hanging out with Wyatt, leading him on when she had no intention of moving beyond that incredible kiss back at Burlesque Bombshells, wasn't fair.

"Why the sad face?" He handed her a steaming mug of coffee.

"Thanks." She took a sip, buying some time before she blurted the truth.

"You didn't answer my question." He sat and gestured at the seat opposite.

"That's because you won't like the answer." She cradled her mug and sat, glad for the distance between them. Because when he'd stood close to her in Chantal's office, she hadn't been able to think and it had been forever since a guy had that kind of effect on her.

"Try me."

Eyeballing him, she said, "I'm not sleeping with you."

She watched for scorn or derision or anger. Instead, his eyes radiated the kind of inscrutable calm that made her want to rattle him to get a reaction.

"I didn't think you would."

Surprised by his response, she bristled. "You didn't?"

He shrugged. "I thought you'd only take the challenge so far and I was right."

Annoyed he had figured her out, she glared. "So you're an IT expert and a psychologist?"

"Nope, just observant." He drank his coffee, staring at her with that all-knowing gaze over the rim of the mug.

It made her uncomfortable, being scrutinized so closely. She wasn't used to it. One of the benefits of being a choreographer and not a dancer on stage.

Increasingly unnerved, she tried defiance. "Don't think you know me, because you wouldn't come close."

She saw a flicker behind his mug, an upturning of his mouth. "Then enlighten me."

Glad to be on safer ground—not talking about why she wouldn't sleep with him despite coming here—she said, "What do you want to know?"

"Everything."

His stare didn't waver and damned if she didn't feel warmth seep through her body. She may not like being studied so intently when he was interrogating her but she didn't mind the way he looked at her now. With admiration, lust and a healthy dose of respect. Not that she'd earned the first and last, but it made her feel good nonetheless.

"I'm twenty-eight, from a small east coast town in Ireland originally, lived in London for a while, choreographed my way across Europe before ending up in Paris, then here." She snapped her fingers. "Oh, and I want world peace."

"Pity you skipped the swimsuit section."

She laughed. "Anything else you want to know?"

"Pet hates. Grand loves. Dirty secrets."

Her smile faded. She had a dirty secret. A doozy. The biggest regret of her life. That had ruined her life. No one in Vegas knew it, even Chantal, and they never would.

So she aimed for flippant. "Hate anchovies. Love honeycomb ice-cream. And the dirty secret?" She crooked her finger. "I'll tell you mine if you tell me yours."

To her surprise, he blushed. "No secrets here."

"Sure?"

"Well, there is one..." He tapped his temple, pretending to think. "Here goes. Kurt got all the girls when we were growing up so I decided to try out for the football team."

"What happened?"

He grimaced. "I ended up being offered the team statistician position."

She laughed out loud at his pained expression. "Girls fancy geeks too, you know."

"Do they?" He placed his coffee cup on a nearby table and braced his elbows on his knees. "More precisely, do you?"

"I'm here, aren't I?" She couldn't resist a coy smile. "Give me a guy with brains over a mimbo any day."

"Mimbo?"

"Male bimbo." She didn't add 'like your brother, Kurt', a pretty boy with an ego the size of Texas to match, according to Chantal.

"Anyway, now you know." He held out his hands, palm up. "No more secrets here."

She wished she could say the same.

"Your turn," he said.

"Hmm...secrets..." She took a sip, another, needing the caffeine hit to jolt her out of the welcome lethargy since she sat in the way-too-comfy chair. "I've got two. Firstly, I'm entering a big competition, for the best choreographer on the western seaboard. And the second one ties into the first." She huffed out a breath. "I'm bored. I love working in Vegas, and I've made some good friends I can count on as a support network, but I feel stagnant. A bit sick of everything, actually. Craving a change but unsure what to do."

Wow, where had all that come from? She'd meant to stop at 'I'm bored' but with him looking at her with empathy and understanding, the truth had poured out.

"Will the competition open new avenues for you?"

No judgment, no smartass remark, just an incredibly insightful question. God, could the guy be any cuter?

She nodded. "Winning will mean prestige and recognition. I could pretty much walk into any job around the world."

"Then I hope you get it." He crossed his fingers, a dorky yet strangely endearing gesture.

"Thanks." She placed her mug on the floor beside her chair. "Do you love what you do?"

"Yeah. Computers have always been my thing, and freelancing is a great way to live."

"Maybe that's why I'm so bored at the moment...staying in one place for so long." She tucked her feet under her, surprisingly comfortable and wondering what made Wyatt so easy to talk to. "That's why I left home in the first place, couldn't stand the small town mentality and the smothering." She shuddered. "I hate living in one place for too long."

"You don't like small towns?"

"Hate them," she said, her vehemence garnering a raised eyebrow.

"Yet you're in a city with bright lights and you're still bored?"

"You make me sound fickle and shallow," she said, stopping her fiddling fingers by clasping them together.

"Didn't mean to," he said. "Maybe you should shake things up to snap out of the boredom funk?"

"How?" She sighed. "Because honestly? If I don't do something soon I'm in danger of quitting my job, packing up and hitting the road."

Something she'd been pondering all too often lately.

"Come home with me," he said, scooting back the moment the invitation spilled from his lips. "I mean, I'm heading home for the weekend. On the outskirts of New Orleans. Small town. I have a quiet place by a bayou. Maybe a change of scenery will reinvigorate you? Or you could do the jazz clubs in New Orleans for a change of pace—"

"Yes." Her acceptance surprised them both, if his round-eyed shock was anything to go by. "That'd be lovely. Thanks."

"Uh...right. Okay." He stood and stalked toward the massive window overlooking The Strip twenty floors below. "Guess we're taking a trip."

"Guess we are."

They stared at each other like two crazy people, a little hesitant and a lot loco.

The fact she'd agreed to spend the weekend with a guy she barely knew in a place that was her version of hell?

She wasn't just crazy.

She was certifiable.

SIX

Wyatt had lost his mind.

For a smart guy, he'd turned into a dumb schmuck last night, asking Ashlin to accompany him on his weekend away. Two precious days at home. His private retreat. His oasis.

That now had a gorgeous woman wearing denim shorts and a red tank top bustling about his kitchen putting away groceries.

What the hell had he been thinking?

He'd never been impulsive. He weighed important decisions, took his time assessing situations objectively. Yet all that had gone to shit last night when he'd blurted that ludicrous invitation because he felt sorry for her.

Worse, she'd actually accepted. She'd hightailed it out of his hotel room a few minutes later, citing she had to pack. And he'd let her go, glad of the reprieve to evaluate what exactly it was about her that made him go a little nuts.

So she was spectacular. He'd dealt with stunning women before—albeit for business—but he'd never been this crazy with any of them. Then again, those women barely looked at him as anything other than a geek to fix their computer woes.

That's what was different about Ashlin. The way she looked at him. Really *looked* at him. Like she could see all the way down to his well-guarded soul. Like she was interested in what he had to say. Like she gave a damn.

Something no one in his life had ever done.

His father didn't give a shit. His mom doted on her firstborn, Kurt, like he'd hung the moon and stars. Neither of them had ever related to him on any level. Wyatt had been the good boy. The one guaranteed to get good grades. The one never in trouble. The one who never caused waves.

As for friends, he'd had none. He'd eaten with fellow computer geeks at school but didn't socialize out of it. He'd lost himself in online games, in tinkering with apps, in building computers from scratch. His make-believe worlds online were his go-to place, where he felt comfortable. And the more he lost himself in his online worlds, the worse his social skills in the real world.

He'd been labeled everything from a hermit to a nerd and worse. He hadn't cared because once he got his degree and started earning the big bucks freelancing he called the shots in his own life. A sought-after guest speaker who commanded respect. Admired at IT conferences. He pulled the chicks there.

And Ashlin was so far from that world that even now he couldn't believe she was here.

He didn't converse with women often, let alone enjoy it. But that's exactly what had happened last night. He'd enjoyed their verbal sparring. He'd admired her honesty. And he'd grown to like her.

Which had to be part of the rationale behind inviting her here. She hated small towns. He lived in one and loved it. So having her out of her comfort zone, seeing how she would probably react badly, would reinforce what he already knew: he couldn't like her. He shouldn't like her. It wouldn't end well.

"You hungry?" She brandished a loaf of crusty bread in one hand and a jar of mustard in the other. "I can whip up some subs."

"Yeah, that'd be great." Would give him time to...what? Crack open a beer as he usually would, fire up the big screen TV and log on to the latest gamer app? He couldn't do that, not with her here, which meant he'd need to entertain her.

Crap.

"Want a beer?"

Great, she could read his mind too. He was in so much trouble. Though at least he could enjoy one of his rituals. "Sure, thanks."

"Bet you didn't think I was a domestic goddess," she said, moving about the kitchen with ease.

"I'll reserve judgment 'til I taste that sub."

"Cynic," she yelled, piling every filling known to man onto the bread, making him salivate. For the sub and the constant peeps at cleavage as she leaned over the counter.

God, she was killing him.

They had all day to get through, tonight, then half a day tomorrow before they headed back to Vegas. Which meant he'd have the worst case of blue balls ever.

Because he was under no illusions: despite her teasing and challenging, Ashlin wasn't giving off the vibes of a woman ready to get down and dirty.

He may not socialize often but he knew the signs of a woman interested in getting naked with him. It had happened five times at conferences. Five different women.

Which is probably what Kurt did in a single night, if rumors were correct. Which made Wyatt inexperienced and out of his depth, but still able to recognize that Ashlin didn't want him the same way he wanted her.

"Here you go." She handed him a plate and a beer. "Dig in."

He waited until she brought hers into the sunroom and sat next to him on the wide three-seater couch before taking a bite.

"Good?"

He managed a mumbled 'yeah' as he silently acknowledged that not only was she gorgeous, she could whip up a gourmet sub from a few ingredients.

"I lived on these things when I first came to America," she said, taking a huge bite out of hers.

And damned if it didn't turn him on, seeing her put something that big in her mouth.

She eyed him speculatively. "Why are you looking at me like that?"

Shit. "I'm still a little off-kilter at seeing you here."

"Why?"

"Because I don't bring people here."

Her jaw dropped a little. "Ever?"

"No." Could he sound any more of a loser?

"So why me?" She lowered her sub to her plate, studying him with an intensity that made him want to head for his man cave.

Fuck, he was already in it.

And so was she.

"Sounded like you needed a break, from what you said last night."

She wrinkled her nose. "That was me being a self-pitying whiner and I have no idea why I told you all that stuff."

"It's good to offload sometimes. Especially to strangers."

He should know. He felt most comfortable with people he barely knew. Hated the intimacy and expectation that came with relationships of any kind.

"So this was a pity invite?"

He needed to say 'of course'. Needed to convince her that he wasn't so hot for her he could hardly see straight. But he saw the wariness in her eyes, like she expected him to kick her when she was down, and he couldn't do it.

He settled for a half-truth. "You intrigue me so that's why I invited you."

Bracing for her to interrogate him further, he sighed in relief when she picked up her sub again.

"I appreciate your honesty," she said, eyeballing him. "Not many guys are."

"You think we're all lying sacks of shit?"

"Mostly." She finished chewing another mouthful. "But you've got this look..."

Great. Here it came. The inevitable 'you look like a nice guy.' Far removed from what he wanted to be with her.

"Dare I ask?"

"You look..." She paused, studying him. "...Like you say what you mean and don't waste time spinning a load of crap."

Her lush mouth curved into a devastating smile that made the few mouthfuls of sub he'd eaten lodge in his gut like a stone. "That's why I accepted your invitation, because I knew you wouldn't have asked if you didn't want me here."

"That's some heavy shit," he said, stuffing his mouth with the sub to prevent from blurting how goddamn right she was.

The rest of the self-talk for the rationale behind his invite had been utter BS. She'd figured him out. He'd invited her to his sanctuary for the simple fact he wanted her here.

"You can handle it." She popped the last of the sub into her mouth and dusted off her fingers.

Maybe. What he couldn't handle was his unrelenting lust for her.

Wishing he could control his libido as easily as statistical data, he said, "What do you want to do after lunch?"

She pointed at the French doors leading from the sunroom to the back porch. "Lie out there with a book. Or fall asleep in that hammock."

It's what he usually did when he returned here on the too few occasions between jobs. Yet another point in her favor. "I thought you were bored? Don't you want to explore the town?"

She shrugged. "Seen one small town, seen them all. I'd rather relax." Her eyes glittered with mischief. "Besides, maybe the company I kept in Vegas bored me and now that I'm here with you...well, let's just say I'm getting less bored by the minute."

"I usually have the opposite effect on women." He gestured at the stack of computer magazines on the coffee table. "Spending time in my company leads to boredom, or so I've been told."

She made a cute *pfft* sound. "Those women were clueless."

"Thanks." He found himself grinning like an idiot before he demolished the remainder of his sub.

"You're welcome." She stood and snagged her beer. "If you're looking for me, I'll be out the back, where that hammock has my name on it."

"Enjoy." Wyatt chugged back his beer, surprised by how contented he felt, listening to the sounds of Ashlin rummaging around the spare room. Watching her pad barefoot across the back porch. Chuckling when it took her three attempts to settle into the hammock without falling on her ass.

He never experienced this type of contentment in the presence of another person. The only time he came close? Grappling and solving complex data problems.

He'd never been a people person.

Maybe letting Ashlin into his life could change all that?

SEVEN

"You know I'm never leaving, right?" Ashlin tucked her feet tighter beneath her, hoping Wyatt couldn't decipher how damn serious she was behind her flippant comment.

It hadn't been the relaxing afternoon spent dozing in the hammock, or the wood-fired pizzas they'd made together while standing side by side in his cozy kitchen, or the old black and white musical they'd watched while sitting within touching distance on the couch that made her want to stay.

Uh-uh, it was the guy who scooted closer, stretched his arm out along the back of the couch, and twisted a strand of her hair around his finger.

Wyatt made her feel at ease, at peace, in a way no one ever had.

She'd been pushing herself for as long as she could remember. First, as a way to prove herself after leaving home. Later, as a way to forget the tragedy that dogged her no matter how hard she tried to forget. She never had vacations. Or took days off. When she traveled, it was to further her career. And on her days off, she watched countless videos of choreographers around the world, honing her skills, inventing new routines.

She never relaxed. And certainly not in the company of a guy.

It made the last twelve hours all the more special. But now she faced the tough stuff. Extricating herself from Wyatt's guaranteed advances because she was too damaged to have sex no matter how much she wanted to.

"Stay as long as you like." His fingertips drifted across the back of her neck, a feather-light caress that made her shiver with longing. "It's good to take time out when you need it."

"I'd need a year's worth of down time to get my head back in the game," she said, wondering what it was about him that made her blurt the truth consistently.

"Want to talk about it?"

His fingers drifted from her neck to her scalp, lightly massaging and she bit back a moan.

"No. No talking..." she said, realizing too late what that sounded like a second before he covered her mouth with his.

God, the guy could kiss. Not too hard. Not too soft. Just right. A slow, sensuous devouring that made her melt into him. Her hands grabbed at his T-shirt, needing an anchor as her world tipped on its axis.

He cradled her head, changing the angle, deepening the kiss until she couldn't think of anything other than being on top of him, skin to skin.

She gripped his T-shirt harder and eased him down on the couch until she lay on top of him. His fingers slipped under her tank top. Unhooked her bra. His hands glided down her back. Cupped her butt. Ground her against him just enough. God, he felt big. And hard.

She couldn't do this, no matter how much she wanted to try. She'd freeze up and disappoint him, and he'd been nothing but lovely to her.

Damn, she never should've let it get this far.

Her cue to run.

But before she could, Wyatt broke the kiss. "Hey, where did you go?"

"Huh?"

"One minute you were into us, the next you were gone." He tapped her temple gently. "Up here."

"Damn you for being so perceptive." She pushed off him, instantly chilled at the loss of body heat. Or more precisely, the loss of him. Because there was nothing surer than him wanting to back off when she told him the partial truth. Something she'd have to do considering how far she'd let things get.

"What did I do?" He scrambled up, his expression a gut-wrenching mix of confusion and regret.

"Nothing, it's not you." She scurried to the furthest corner of the couch and hugged her knees to her chest. "I'm screwed up about sex."

A crease dented his forehead. "We were just making out. Doesn't have to lead to anything—"

"But I want it to for the first time in forever, because it's you and you're great and sweet and hot, but I can't, and it's so damn shitty..." she trailed off, unaware she'd been screeching until she saw him gaping at her. "Sorry, it's beyond frustrating."

If he said, 'sure, I understand,' she'd throw something at him. Because no one understood what she'd gone through and how it affected her ability to get physical. The counselor at the hospital had said her body would repair over time and she'd be able to resume intimate relations. But what about how badly it had screwed with her head?

"I want to help but I have no fucking clue how to." To his credit, Wyatt kept his distance. He didn't stare at her with pity, which would've undone her completely. Instead, he looked at her like he cared.

And that unlocked her heart a little more.

"I went through something major after I left home. It left me pretty screwed up sexually."

She glimpsed a flicker of horror in his wide eyes and rushed on, "I wasn't raped or abused or anything. But ever since, I don't enjoy sex."

His shoulders relaxed, his relief evident. "Feel free to tell me to shut the fuck up if this is too personal, but can you come?"

Shocked to her core that she'd revealed so much, she shook her head.

"Hmm..." Rather than stare at her, he looked off into space, as if contemplating some giant cosmic puzzle and for the first time in the last few minutes, she felt like laughing.

"What are you thinking?"

"Let me help." His gaze met hers and his sincerity blew her away. "Sure, I want to get in your pants. I mean, which guy wouldn't, you're that smoking hot. But maybe we leave the intercourse for later and concentrate on getting you off."

Wow. He wanted to *help*? His thoughtfulness blew her away. She'd imagined him running for the nearest bayou after she told him yet here he was, not judging her, not ridiculing her, but present in a way no guy had ever been.

But what shocked her the most? She actually trusted him enough to want to try.

"When you put it like that, how can a girl resist?"

He smiled at her dry response. "How many times have you had sex since that stuff in your past?"

Heat scorched her cheeks. "I've tried three times over the years but never made it past the kissing stage."

"Shit," he muttered, quickly masking his shock by rubbing a hand over his face.

"So there's no pressure on you or anything," she said, trying to alleviate the mood, touched and confused and hopeful by his offer to help her through this. "I'm frigid. You think you can help. Maybe we should give it a shot?"

He nodded, his expression still thoughtful. "Though I should warn you. I've been with a grand total of five women so I'm probably not the sex-god you expect."

His honesty made her want to hold him tight.

"Well, that's four people more than I've ever been with, so you'll have more of a clue than I will."

His open-mouthed shock was comical. "You've only been with one guy?"

She nodded. "So now you know everything."

Not quite everything, but she'd revealed enough secrets for one night.

He held out his hand and after several long drawn out moments, she took it. "Do you trust me?"

She bit back her first response of 'I barely know you'. Because she wouldn't have shared so much of herself if she didn't trust him and somewhere deep inside, on an instinctive level, she'd never felt so safe as she did with Wyatt.

"I trust you."

"Then let's take this one step at a time. Real slow." He squeezed her hand, before lifting it to his lips and brushing a soft kiss on the back. "You in?"

Ashlin had never let any guy get close since Dougal. Her first love. The guy who had changed her life and then left without looking back after what she'd done. She'd never been interested in intimacy since. Too painful, too emotionally draining, to confront the truth: that the decision she'd made back then had effectively ruined her chances of ever feeling close to anyone again.

But she'd told Wyatt some of the truth and he was still here. More astonishing, he was willing to help her work through some of her issues. She'd be a fool to say no.

She eyeballed the incredibly sensitive, understanding guy. "I'm in all the way."

EIGHT

After Ashlin's big revelation, Wyatt poured them a double shot of brandy. Alcohol would help ease the jitters. It had to.

What the fuck was he thinking, volunteering to help a woman he barely knew explore her sexuality like he was some kind of frigging expert?

Shit, this stuff was more up Kurt's alley. Then again, Kurt would've walked away so fast from Ashlin after her admission that her head would've spun.

Exactly what he should've done.

He'd never been chivalrous or tuned in to women before. Thanks to an extensive repertoire of porn in his late teens, he'd figured out how to get the business done with a woman, ensuring they were both happy. But five sexual encounters did not a Romeo make and he had no fucking clue why he'd offered to help Ashlin through this.

But then she flashed him a tentative smile over the rim of her brandy balloon and something unexpected twanged in his chest, giving him enough of a clue as to why.

He liked her.

Really liked her.

She was different from the other women he'd been with. A tough outer core hiding a flawed, vulnerable woman. The kind of woman who reached to him on a deeper level than he could fathom.

Emotions were alien to him. He didn't love. He liked things. Liked his job, his brother, his new half-brothers, his house. He might even like his parents, despite the shitty job they'd done with him. But he'd never felt anything beyond like. Never a deep connection that signaled a possible undoing of his neat, factual world.

He didn't like mess or complications. Yet the longer Ashlin stared at him with those guileless blue eyes, the more he knew he could be heading for both.

"Second guessing your offer?"

That was another thing. The way she honed in on his thoughts. All the time.

"A little." He drained the brandy, desperately wanting a top up but needing his wits about him. "I'm thinking I may be in over my head."

To his surprise, Ashlin laughed. "God, I love how refreshingly honest you are." She placed her half empty glass on the table. "It makes me like you all the more."

Wyatt could've sworn an air bubble had expanded in his chest. "You like me?"

"Yeah. I feel comfortable around you." Her fingertips grazed his hand. "Considering I don't let anyone get too close, that's a pretty big deal for me."

Their similarities startled him. "I'm the same. And I feel the same. With you." Hell, could he sound any goofier?

She smiled and intertwined her fingers with his, which

he took as a good sign considering how fast she'd jumped off him ten minutes ago. "I think fate is a crock, but maybe we met for a reason."

"You're right, it's a crock," he said, but he squeezed her hand. "So here's how I see this playing out. You've got that big competition coming up. I've got another two weeks work at Burlesque Bombshells. Why don't we hang out in our spare time? Have some fun." He paused, and traced a slow circle in her palm, enjoying the way her pupils dilated in response. "And take a real shot at making fireworks in the bedroom."

"And I was just hoping for a good, old-fashioned orgasm or ten." She deadpanned, before flinging herself into his arms and hugging him so tight he could barely breathe. "Thanks. For everything."

"I haven't given you an everything or ten yet," he said, burying his face in her hair and breathing deeply, savoring the exotic, spicy scent that he'd already come to associate with her.

She buried her head in the crook of his neck and giggled. "At this point in time, I'd settle for one."

"Then shall we get started?"

She stiffened slightly in his arms as it struck him again, what a colossal idiot he was for thinking he could do this.

"Sure." She wriggled back, but held onto his hands. "What did you have in mind?"

Ignoring the growing sense of doom, he rested their hands on his knees. "Tell me your erogenous zones."

She swallowed, took her time answering. "I'm not sure."

"Then it's my job to find out." He released her hands and slid away from her, patting his lap. "Pop your feet up here."

He swore he glimpsed a flicker of disappointment in her nervous gaze and that vindicated his choice of what he was about to do. It meant she'd expected him to go straight for the good stuff but that wasn't how this would work.

He knew enough about women to know that foreplay was everything. Women orgasmed with their minds, not just their bodies. Luckily, he was good with minds. Facts. Logic.

So logically, he'd build anticipation. Give her the longest, drawn-out foreplay she'd ever had. Make her want an orgasm so bad that she'd be unable to hold it back when he finally did hone in on the spot he'd give anything to be licking right now.

"You've got a naughty look on your face," she said, gasping when he pressed his thumb into the arch of her foot.

"That's because I'm imagining doing some incredibly naughty things to you," he said, dragging his thumb upward toward her toes. Kneading their bases. Relieved as she moaned and wriggled and sighed.

Her smug little smile indicated they were off to a good start.

He focused on her right foot first. Long, firm strokes. Pulling on her toes. Tracing her arch. Making her squirm. Before lavishing the same on her left foot.

She made the cutest noises, half way between a groan and a grunt. And with her eyes half-closed, the lids heavy with passion, it took every ounce of willpower for Wyatt to stop at touching her feet.

"That feels so good...*ooooh*..." She actually lifted her pelvis off the couch a tad as he squeezed the base of her Achilles tendon and his cock throbbed in response.

"Imagine how my hands will feel all over your body."

With that, he released her feet, pushed them off his lap and stood. "Goodnight."

He didn't dare look back, because if he saw a glimpse of her wanting him as badly as he wanted her, he wouldn't be able to stick to his plan of taking things slow.

Damn, logic was a bitch sometimes.

NINE

Ashlin hadn't slept.

At all.

Thanks to that bloody Wyatt, who'd left her wanting more.

She knew it was a good thing. Her feeling anything more than disinterest when a guy touched her. But Wyatt's foot massage shouldn't have felt so sexual. Yet it had. Which begged the question, what had changed?

Was it a simple matter of logistics; it had been so long since she'd had an orgasm with a guy that any touch would do?

She doubted it. She'd never been short of offers to scratch that proverbial itch over the years but with those guys they'd never passed first base because she hadn't felt anything.

With Wyatt, she felt *everything*. Too much. Too soon. And it was oh too tempting. She'd wanted to take it further last night. Had wanted him to slide those strong, masterful hands up her calves, along her thighs and higher, assuaging the throb that persisted long into the night.

But she'd been scared. Terrified, in fact, that she'd freeze up like she usually did when anyone other than herself got in the vicinity. She could masturbate to orgasm but if the guys she'd kissed groped the area, nothing. Not that the orgasms she gave herself could be counted as anything less than serviceable. She got off. Barely. Felt a little zing, released tension. Similar to drinking a virgin margarita: quenched thirst without the buzz.

She hadn't got herself off last night because she wanted to savor the feelings Wyatt had elicited. Had wanted to remember them for whenever he took things further. And he would. She had no doubt.

He'd played it just right, leaving her wanting and yearning.

And anticipating what he'd come up with next.

"Good morning." He came up behind her and brushed a soft kiss beneath her ear.

"Is it?" She squealed as he nipped the skin at the base of her neck. "Okay, it is."

"So you're not in a snit after I left you hanging last night?" He perched on the verandah railing, looking incredibly delectable in khaki cargo shorts and a white T. "Because you realize it's for the greater good?"

"I'm not a complete moron," she said, wondering if she should be annoyed by his smugness but deciding it wasn't worth the effort.

She'd come clean about her frigidity last night. She couldn't hide behind coyness now. Too late for that.

"You enjoyed the foot massage?"

"You know I did." To her surprise, heat flooded her cheeks. Way too late for blushes too.

"Good, because there's more where that came from." He slid off the railing and held out his hand to her. "Fancy a walk along the bayou, followed by beignets and cafe au lait?"

"Now you're really upping the torture." She slid her hand into his, loving how right it felt. "I'd do anything for a beignet."

"Anything?" His low, suggestive tone sent a sizzle of heat through her.

"Try me and find out."

He ducked down to whisper in her ear. "I intend to, and guaranteed I won't need a beignet to do it."

That damn heat zeroed in on the one area that surprisingly responded to him and made her ache with wanting to head back inside and let him try her out for real.

"Come on, I'm starving." She bumped him with her hip and he jostled her back.

And they kept up the playfulness as they strolled along the banks of the bayou bordering his property. A pinch here. A swat on the ass there. And lots of loaded glances that threatened to scorch her clothes off.

By the time they made it to the tiny corner store, Ashlin wanted to forego the beignets in favor of a quickie in the nearby marshland.

"Here, you'll need sustenance." He handed her a beignet warm from the oven and a coffee.

"For?"

"To keep up your strength, of course." He raised his coffee cup to her. "I plan on driving you to the brink repeatedly over the next two weeks."

She swallowed her coffee so fast it burned her throat. "You sure know how to get a girl all hot and bothered."

"That's the idea, sweetheart." His lips grazed hers. Once. Twice. Before his tongue tangled with hers all too briefly.

He tasted of sugar and cinnamon and coffee, three of her favorite things.

When he eased away, she practically swooned. Slightly embarrassed by her over the top reaction to him, she took a massive bite out of a beignet. And almost swooned again.

"That good, huh?"

"Heaven," she mumbled, devouring the rest while he looked on with a bemused grin.

"Sweetheart, if I can put the same kind of expression on your face as that pastry just did, I'll be a happy man indeed." He tapped the end of her nose. "Icing sugar right here."

"You've got some on your lip." She hauled him close and ran her tongue along his bottom lip, enjoying his sharp intake of breath. Glad she wasn't the only one affected by their flirting.

"You know you're killing me, right?" He lobbed his coffee cup in the trash and dusted off his hands.

"You're the one who wants to take things real slow."

"For *your* benefit."

"That's right." She snapped her fingers. "There's a flaw in your dastardly plan."

"What?"

"In driving me insane with longing, you're going to do the same to yourself."

With that, she slapped him on the ass and sauntered away, whistling a sultry dance tune and grinning as she heard a frustrated growl behind her.

ASHLIN SLEPT the whole way back to Vegas and Wyatt was glad.

Keeping up the banter was exhausting.

Not because he didn't enjoy it. He did. But having

Ashlin constantly touch him, albeit playfully, and stare at him, and smile at him...well, he was having a damn hard time focusing on the logic of his dumbass plan.

He wanted her with a ferocity that scared the hell out of him. He fantasized constantly: what she'd look like naked. Would her bush be as red as her hair? Would her nipples be pink or brown? Would she be as flexible as he hoped because of her job? It was driving him frigging nuts.

So he'd been a chicken-shit and dropped her at Burlesque Bombshells when she'd cited some rehearsal issue, and had hightailed it to Zane's hotel. Another dumbass move, considering his half-brother had moved out of his suite and into Chantal's apartment last week.

However, just as he put the hire car back into gear, Steele stepped out of the foyer and waved.

Wyatt hesitated. He barely knew the guy and while Steele had given him some good advice regarding Ashlin, he wasn't up for discussing everything that had gone down over the weekend with a virtual stranger.

But then he glimpsed Steele's crestfallen expression and guilt kicked in. The guy had flown half way around the world, would be gone in a month and it wasn't Steele's fault that his half-brother feared socializing.

Wyatt pulled over and got out. "Hey. What are you up to?"

"Going for a walk." Steele sauntered over, like nothing fazed him. But Wyatt saw the restrained energy in his posture, in the set of his shoulders. Steele would be a go-getter and he admired that.

"Change that to a beer and I'll stick around," Wyatt said.

Steele laughed. "You're on. Besides, you stood me up for that drink yesterday."

"Sorry, had to duck home for a few days," Wyatt said. "Didn't you get my text?"

"Yeah, no worries."

They headed into the hotel bar, ordered drinks, and Wyatt felt the familiar pressure to say something, anything, rather than sit silent like a dork.

If Steele noticed any awkwardness, he didn't show it. "So where's home for you?"

"Small town on the outskirts of New Orleans. It's peaceful."

"You value peace, huh?"

Not sure how to respond, Wyatt nodded.

"You strike me as the quiet type, that's all."

Steele's astuteness impressed him. "When it comes to talking, less is more."

"I'll drink to that." They clinked beer bottles. "Does Kurt subscribe to the same way of thinking?"

Wyatt snorted. "You can't shut the bastard up, especially if he's talking about himself. Why?"

A frown appeared between Steele's brows. "Because he sent me a text. Short and sweet. Suggesting we meet up when he's in town in two weeks."

Wyatt knew Kurt would be intimidated, having his position as eldest son usurped by the Aussie, so Kurt extending the hand of friendship to Steele amazed him. Particularly when Kurt usually never gave a shit about anyone but himself.

"You seem surprised?" Steele said.

"Word of advice. Kurt and Christopher are like this." He intertwined his first and middle fingers. "So Christopher may use him to meet you."

Steele's frown deepened. "I'm not interested in anything

the old man has to say and I'll tell him to his face if he ever dared confront me."

"He'll dare," Wyatt said. "Christopher has a hide thick as a rhino. And the curiosity will be killing him, so he'll definitely do something underhanded to get to you."

"Prick," Steele muttered, downing most of his beer in a few gulps.

Not wanting to waste time talking about Christopher, Wyatt changed the subject. "Ashlin came home with me."

Steele's eyebrows shot heavenward. "The redhead?"

Wyatt nodded and Steele whistled low. "Wow. There are no flies on you, mate."

"Did you just insult me?"

Steele sniggered. "It's an Aussie saying, means you're astute. Switched on."

Frigging turned on, more like it, but Wyatt couldn't share that much with his half-brother.

Steele stared at him with admiration. "So what happened?"

"I did what you said. Called her bluff. Next thing I know I asked her to come home for the weekend and she accepted. We hung out. Got to know each other. It was nice." Could he sound any lamer?

"Nice?" Steele jabbed him in the chest. "Mate, nice is for cupcakes and puppies." He grinned. "I'm hoping for your sake it moved beyond nice."

"We fooled around a little." Wyatt wouldn't say anything more than that and Steele must've picked up on his recalcitrant vibe, because he nodded and didn't pry.

"Good for you." Steele slapped him on the back. "She's a stunner."

Wyatt managed a weak, "Yeah," before hiding behind his beer bottle again.

He could ask Steele's advice, but what Ashlin had revealed to him was private and he didn't want to encroach on that. Besides, if her demeanor this morning had been any indication, his plan to make her so hot she'd beg for it was working. The sexual tension between them was palpable. And he intended on ratcheting that up later today.

"Will you see her again?"

"Yeah, we're going to date casually while I'm in Vegas."

Looking suitably impressed, Steele gestured at the barman. "Another round?"

"Nah, I'm good, thanks." Wyatt also wanted to move onto phase two of his plan and that meant heading back to his hotel suite. "I've actually got to catch up on work tonight. Maybe we can organize a dinner with Zane sometime this week?"

"Sounds like a plan." Steele picked up his refill. "Catch you later."

"Okay." Wyatt wasn't the touchy-feely type. He rarely shook hands with Kurt. Yet for some inexplicable reason he felt like giving Steele a man-hug. The guy looked lonely.

Steele shot him a curious glance when he hadn't move, so Wyatt raised his hand and walked away. The person he should be considering touching was Ashlin.

Sooner rather than later.

TEN

"Where did you disappear to over the weekend?" Miranda linked her hands and stretched overhead. "Even Chantal noticed your absence and that's saying something considering she's shacked up with Lover Boy and not coming up for air."

"I went away." Ashlin dabbed at her face with a towel then draped it around her neck.

When she'd asked Wyatt to drop her off at Burlesque Bombshells, she'd envisaged a leisurely work out session by herself. Sunday nights were notoriously quiet at the club, with the dancers performing two brief shows and the place closing early.

Chantal had wanted that from the beginning, to give her staff some down time one day a week and her employees appreciated it. Ashlin rarely had input into the Sunday shows, the dancers performing the same routine for as long as she could remember. Mainly regulars came in on Sundays. They knew what to expect and the girls delivered. The ever-popular fan dance. One of the girls in a life-sized champagne glass. A combo veil-feather number.

It meant Ashlin could have a complete night off. She'd usually curl up with a book. Tonight, she'd needed to work off her frustrations.

She hadn't counted on running into Miranda in the club's gym.

"Where'd you go?" Miranda moved onto stretching her quads and hamstrings.

"A town near New Orleans."

"Nice. Spa retreat?"

"No, a friend's house." Ashlin eyed the door, wondering if she could escape before Miranda's interrogation continued.

Her friend loved to gossip and Ashlin would bear the brunt if Miranda learned any more.

"Anyway, I have to run—"

"Anyone I know?" Miranda lunged to one side and held the stretch, the twinkle in her eyes alerting Ashlin to the fact she wouldn't let up until she knew every last nitty gritty detail.

"No." Ashlin picked up her workout bag and slung it over her shoulder. "See you later—"

"Male or female friend?"

Knowing she was sunk, Ashlin shrugged. "Male."

Miranda abandoned her stretching and bounded over. "Tell me more."

"Nothing to tell. Wyatt asked me to go with him and—"

"Wyatt!" Miranda screeched, and Ashlin wondered if the audience had heard from all the way across the club's complex. "The cutie fixing our computers?"

Ashlin nodded, knowing she wouldn't have to say another word, as Miranda would continue to babble with excitement.

"But I didn't know you two were even dating. And for

him to ask you to go away with him, that's huge." Miranda rubbed her hands together. "And obviously Chantal doesn't know. Wow, you two could be sisters-in-law—"

"Whoa. Hold on there. We're just dating while he's in town, that's it."

Miranda, a hopeless romantic who lived on a diet of erotic novels and rom-com movies, clasped her hands to her heart. "It's so great. You've been single for ages and he's lovely so imagine if you did get together long-term—"

"You're hopeless." Ashlin laughed and headed for the door. "Go home and read one of those smutty books you love and leave me alone."

"I want details!" Miranda yelled and Ashlin flipped her the bird.

As Ashlin slipped out of the door, her cell buzzed with an incoming message.

She rummaged in her bag and pulled it out, knowing Miranda worked fast but not that fast. This couldn't be Chantal demanding Intel on her weekend away.

When she saw the sender's name on the screen, her heart did a weird little skive.

WOT R U WEARING?

Was Wyatt trying to have phone sex with her? One way to find out.

She typed a response: PINK THONG. C-THRU LACE BRA.

The message had barely entered cyberspace when he answered.

TAKE THEM OFF.

Heat flushed her cheeks. Wow, she'd never had phone sex before. And the anticipation of doing it with Wyatt made her hands shake.

She bolted for her office, slammed the door shut and

flicked the lock. She slipped off her sneakers and made herself comfortable on the small two-seater sofa opposite her desk. Then she answered.

NOT TIL U GET NAKED 1ST.

She stared at her cell's screen, willing a return message. When it came, she jumped.

DONE. NOW U.

Feeling foolish, Ashlin unhooked her bra and pulled it through the sleeve of her tank top. Then she shimmied out of her thong and put her shorts back on. She may be up for her first bout of phone sex but no way could she lounge around her office naked.

Her cell pinged. PINCH NIPPLES. ROLL THEM. IMAGINE IT'S ME.

Ashlin placed the cell on the sofa next to her, and did as Wyatt instructed. It felt good. Fantastic, in fact. Imagining his fingers tweaking the hardened nubs.

TOUCH YOUR CLIT.

She didn't need to be asked twice, the pressure building as she looked down and envisaged Wyatt's head between her legs. Imagined entwining her fingers in his dark curls as his tongue licked her...

FASTER. LIKE I'M PUMPING MY COCK.

Seeing his explicitness on the screen had her excitement skyrocketing. She circled her clit with her middle finger, faster and faster, her breathing shallow.

Sweat beaded between her breasts, trickled down to where she couldn't stop staring at her hand. Until her cell beeped again and she eagerly glanced at it to see Wyatt's next instruction.

U R SO WET 4 ME. CUM.

And she did, the spasms stronger than anything she'd ever experienced alone, draining every last drop of energy as she sank deeper into the sofa cushions.

Every inch of her body tingled, like being zapped with tiny bursts of electricity. Hell, if Wyatt could do this remotely, she could be ready sooner than expected to let him try it for real.

She picked up her cell, lost for words. It vibrated in her hand.

SWEET DREAMS. C U SOON.

That was it? She wanted more. Now.

But considering how goddamn horny Wyatt had made her over the weekend, the guy knew what he was doing. She needed to trust him. Something she'd never done with any guy since Dougal.

So she responded with XXX. Three kisses that could be interpreted as X-rated.

After all, why should she be the only one left squirming?

ELEVEN

Wyatt didn't contact Ashlin for two days.

Making her wait almost killed him.

He worked remotely too, not daring to enter Burlesque Bombshells on the off chance he'd run into her. If he did he wouldn't be responsible for his actions.

There was a difference between patience and insanity, and he trod a fine line between the two. He wanted to build the anticipation for her, but in turn it drove him frigging nuts.

He couldn't wait any longer.

He would invite her over tonight. Time for this seduction to move on from feet and texting to...more.

As he picked up his cell to text her, an incoming videoconference call on his PC lit up.

Kurt.

Not in the mood for his brother's usual brash crap, he hesitated. Then a memory of Steele's questions popped into his head and he did the right thing.

He answered and Kurt's big head and wide shoulders filled the screen. "Hey bozo."

"Hey putz." Kurt grinned like he didn't have a care in the world. That grin irked. "What are you doing?"

"Work. You know, that thing I do for a living, rather than chase a pigskin around a park while trying to dodge a bunch of Neanderthals."

"Still jealous of my athletic prowess, I see."

Wyatt scowled. "Bite me."

Kurt's grin faded. "How are the Aussies?"

Ah, so that's what this call was about. Wyatt knew he should be glad Kurt showed an interest in their half-brothers. Then again, shouldn't he be calling them? Typical Kurt, ignoring him until he needed something. Using him, calling him to pave the way.

So he decided to rub it in a little. "Zane's great. Moved in with Chantal. And Steele's a good guy. Dynamo businessman. We've been hanging out."

He could've sworn Kurt paled a little beneath his year-round tan. "He's doing business while he's here?"

Touchdown. Wyatt bit back a grin. "Nah. But he does marketing for all the big brands around the world. He's the best at what he does."

Kurt mumbled, "Uh-huh," before his lips compressed into a thin line.

Wyatt felt bad for baiting him, for all of two seconds before he remembered the countless times Kurt had taunted him.

"I'm coming to Vegas in a few days and I want us all to hang out," Kurt blurted, sounding uncharacteristically anxious. "I'll throw a party. Less pressure that way."

"Okay." He had to give Kurt some credit. The brother he'd grown up with didn't go out of his way very often, and the fact he wanted to spend time with his siblings was a big deal. "See you then."

Kurt saluted, about to sign off, when Wyatt added, "Don't invite Christopher."

Kurt instantly glanced away and Wyatt's heart sank. "Tell me he didn't set you up to do this as a way to meet Steele."

"Fuck, no. What do you take me for?"

"Daddy's golden boy," Wyatt said, with more than a hint of rancor. "Look, Steele remembers Christopher. He remembers a father who upped and left him to start another family, then didn't contact him again. He's come all this way to meet us. Don't rub his nose in it."

After a long pause, Kurt nodded. "I'll think about it."

"You do that." Wyatt hit the end-call button before he said anything he'd regret. Such as telling Kurt what it felt like to be a son ignored by his father. To feel inadequate and never good enough. To feel an outcast in his own frigging family.

Fuck, if Wyatt felt all those things and he'd had Christopher around, how much worse must it have been for Steele?

Hopefully Kurt had got the message and Christopher wouldn't be at his party.

For all their sakes.

ASHLIN DIDN'T LIKE HOTELS. She'd lived in enough of them while touring around Europe and the novelty had grown old fast. And she particularly hated room service. She'd spent too many nights eating in her hotel room because she had to keep up her strength, followed by crying jags that left her wishing she hadn't eaten a thing.

Those days had been the pits personally, while professionally she'd gained a reputation as an innovative choreographer with the capability of producing unique, standout routines. She'd been revered in public. And filled with self-loathing in private.

When she'd initially fled her home and ended up in trouble in London, she'd done what she had to do at the time. It had been her sole option. But Dougal hadn't seen it that way and she'd lost him too. She'd been an emotional wreck. But dance had saved her and it would ultimately save her now.

The big competition had been moved forward to this Thursday, two days from now. She was ready. Had rehearsed with the girls a million times. Yet she couldn't ignore the ever-present niggle at the back of her mind: what if she didn't win? What then? Would she continue to stagnate in Vegas, reluctant to take a chance on something new?

Shaking off her thoughts, she fixed a smile on her face as Wyatt served dessert. Chocolate mousse. Signature room service fare.

He faltered, the plate perched precariously on his palm. "You don't like mousse?"

"I'm not a fan of room service," she said, wishing she didn't feel compelled to enunciate every honest thought around this guy.

A puzzled frown creased his brow. "Why didn't you say something? We could've gone out to eat?"

She took the plate, placed it on the coffee table and pressed a kiss to his palm. "Because I wouldn't have been able to do that in public."

His eyes darkened to ebony. "If it's confession time, I have to admit I invited you here to say screw the plan and let me screw you."

She smiled at his bluntness. "That phone sex was pretty intense, huh?"

"Hell yeah." He sat next to her, temptingly close. "Think I'm torturing myself more than you."

"I'm being tortured plenty." She fanned her face. "You make me incredibly hot."

"Ditto." He sat next to her, their knees touching. "But I don't want to ruin this." He laid a hand on her thigh and she could've sworn her skin sizzled through the thin cotton dress she'd worn. "I'd planned on sending you steamy emails and handwritten notes and all sorts of smutty stuff."

"And now?"

"Now I just want you."

His sincerity floored her.

She'd never met anyone like him. Honest. Genuine. Not afraid to articulate exactly what he thought.

She covered his hand with hers. "I'm willing to give this a try if you are."

"I think you're amazing," he said, never breaking eye contact as he turned his hand over and threaded his fingers through hers. "And I'm honored you want to try this with me."

Damned if tears didn't well up in her eyes and she blinked rapidly. "I'm the lucky one," she said, leaning forward to press a kiss to his lips. "Thanks for being so patient with me."

She heard him murmur, "You're worth the wait," as he stood and gently tugged her to her feet.

They didn't speak as they walked hand in hand into the bedroom. When she caught sight of the bed, a little frisson of fear slithered through her. What if she disappointed him? And herself, yet again?

She'd come so far. Was it worth dredging up the inevitable feelings of inadequacy?

"We'll take this slow," he said, switching off the lights so the neon from The Strip many floors below bathed the room in a gentle glow.

"Okay." She didn't move as he grabbed the hem of his polo shirt and peeled it overhead.

Held her breath as he undid the button on his jeans and unzipped, pushed the denim down his legs and stepped out of them.

Curled her fingers into her palms as he toyed with the elastic of his boxers.

"Don't stop," she whispered, not wanting to break the spell that had enveloped her the moment he started to strip.

With his skin dappled in colored light, his leanness accentuated by zero body fat, and enough muscles to make her fingers itch with wanting to explore, he was breathtaking.

"All the way, huh?" He eased the boxers down, and her breath caught.

He was big. Thick. And jutting toward her with pride.

"You're beautiful," she said, finally gaining the courage to move.

If this guy could strip for her, she could do the same.

But as she popped the first button on her skirt, she stilled. He'd see the scars. He'd know. And he'd judge her, like she judged herself every freaking day.

"What's wrong?" He took a step toward her and she held up her hands. Yeah, like that would ward off the sight of that much perfection.

"Can we do this my way for now?" Her hands dropped to her sides as she crossed the short space between them. "I want this to be about you tonight."

A tiny frown creased his brow. "Do you want to stop?"

"No." She knelt in front of him, heard his sharp intake of breath.

"Babe, you don't have to—"

"I want to." Glancing up at him, she said, "Please?"

"Fuck," he muttered, looking more tortured by the minute. "As if I'm going to say no."

She smiled and flicked her tongue out, grazing the tip of his penis.

"Oh man..." He rested his hand lightly on her head. "But I want to please you."

"This will please me." She wrapped her hand around the base of his cock and squeezed lightly. "Besides, the more horny I get the better, right?"

He managed a garbled response as she sucked him into her mouth. Swirled her tongue around him. Licked up one side of his shaft and down the other. Alternating speed. Faster. Slower. Her hand pumping him at the same time as she sucked.

"Fuck, that feels good." His hand fisted her hair, tugging on her scalp, urging her on. She didn't need the encouragement. Blowing Wyatt made her throb with wanting him and to give him pleasure empowered her like nothing else.

As she picked up tempo she cradled his balls with her free hand, tugging lightly, using her thumb to press just behind.

He came on a load groan, his final frenetic thrusts making her jaw ache. She didn't care, as Wyatt withdrew and sank to the floor in front of her.

He cradled her face, staring at her like she'd given him the greatest gift on earth. "That was incredible. Thank you."

"You're welcome." Oddly shy with the way he kept staring at her, she wriggled back a little. "Do you mind if I leave?"

Surprise flickered in his eyes as he opened his mouth to

respond and she pressed a finger to his lips. "I've got the big competition in two days and I need to get some sleep."

"You can sleep here," he said, gesturing at the bed. "I don't snore, if that's what you're worried about."

"I'm more worried about being unable to resist you and being kept up all night." She cupped his cheek. "I know I keep blowing hot and cold. And I seriously wanted to go all the way with you tonight. But most of my problem? Up here." She tapped her head. "And I need to focus on us one hundred percent when we end up in bed, not have my mind wandering."

He grimaced. "You think I'll be that bad?"

"I think you'll be stupendous." She kissed him. "But I'm the one who's a screw up so I need my head in the game."

His mouth downturned a little. "Don't take this the wrong way, but have you ever thought over-analyzing could be making it worse? That you need to stop thinking and start feeling?" He palmed her breast, tweaked her nipple through her top. "Too much assessing may be making you tense?"

"You're probably right." Though it was so much more complicated than that. If only it was as simple as turning off her voice of reason and going with the flow. "But I need to leave."

He hesitated, before nodding, his reluctance to let her go obvious. "Okay. I'll give you a few days to get your competition out of the way."

He stood and helped her to her feet. "But after that, sweetheart? It's no holds barred."

TWELVE

High on post-comp adrenalin, and the certainty she'd nailed it, Ashlin bounced into Burlesque Bombshells, eager to tell the girls how she'd done so she could catch up with Wyatt ASAP.

He'd given her the space she'd asked for, with no contact bar a brief text this morning wishing her luck. But that hadn't stopped her thinking about him almost every second of every day. It hadn't been so bad when she'd been rehearsing her ass off but the last few nights, after she'd gone to bed early, he was all she could think about.

She'd missed him. Missed him in a way that made her edgy and uncomfortable.

She didn't need an emotional connection with the guy trying to get her rocks off, but that's exactly what had happened. Because she didn't miss Wyatt's flirting or physical attention. She missed *him*. The way he made her feel with his attentiveness. The way he said what he meant. The way he looked at her, like nothing she could say or do would disappoint him.

How wrong he was.

As she entered her office to drop off her bag, she spied a cascade of flowers on her desk.

Not a bunch of flowers. No cliché roses. But an exquisite cream ceramic pot, covered in turquoise swirls, with an orchid plant in it. And not just any orchid. A four-foot high plant with pale pink orchids tumbling from stems.

It must've cost a fortune, but that wasn't what had her heart sinking.

A potted plant signaled permanency. Something she couldn't throw away, not like a bunch of flowers that withered and died within a week or two.

And if there was one thing she didn't want in her life right now, it was to be stuck in anything resembling permanent.

She reached for the card, knowing it had to be from Wyatt. A permanent kind of guy. His house in a small town pretty much proved that.

Hell, was he becoming too invested in them? Did he want more?

Nothing he'd said had indicated as much. Two weeks, casual dating, had been his stipulation. But Wyatt was a thinker. What if he'd been thinking too much about them?

She slipped the card from the envelope and stared at the embossed words.

CONGRATS ON NAILING THE COMPETITION.

NOW STOP THINKING, TAKE TIME TO SMELL THE ORCHIDS, RELAX AND LET'S TAKE THE NEXT STEP.

Her breath caught. The next step? Oh no, as she suspected, Wyatt wanted more than she was willing to give.

The card slipped from her fingers and as she grabbed it,

it flipped over. Revealing more words. That made her laugh out loud in relief.

AND THAT NEXT STEP IS NAILING YOU.

She laughed so hard her abdominals twanged. The card was so Wyatt. Serious tinged with humor. Thoughtful, yet blunt.

And she wanted him more than ever.

A knock sounded at the door and she yelled, "Come in."

Expecting Chantal or Miranda, she slipped the card back into the envelope and tucked it into the base of the plant, glancing up when she heard the door close and the lock flick.

"So did you?" Wyatt propped against the door, a quintessential hipster in tight denim, white T and caramel suede bomber jacket. "Nail the comp?"

"I did." She couldn't keep the smug grin off her face.

"Then I guess it's time to nail you." He advanced toward her, the determination in his greedy stare as he devoured her from top to bottom making her chest tighten.

"Here?" It came out a squeak.

"I can't wait any longer," he said, his hands spanning her waist. "Staying away from you these last two days have killed me and I'm done taking cold showers."

Turned on by this new take-charge Wyatt, she tossed her hair back. "What happened to this being all about me? About making me wait?"

"Fuck that." He hoisted her onto the desk. "I'm just as guilty as you of over-analyzing, so let's change the plan." He stepped between her legs. "Starting now."

Before she could answer his mouth covered hers, hard and demanding. No more gentle coaxing. No teasing. Wyatt kissed her with the pent-up frustration of a guy who wanted her. Here and now.

Their tongues tangled as he nudged her knees apart. He grabbed her butt and dragged it to the edge of the desk. Pressed her clit against his hardness.

She moaned as he ground against her, his tongue plunging into her mouth, mimicking what she wanted him to do to her.

He tore his mouth from hers, his eyes wild as he unzipped her workout sweatshirt, almost tearing it in his haste to get it off her.

She shrugged out of it, tossed it aside, her pulse skyrocketing as his mouth fixed on a nipple through the cotton of her sports bra. He bit gently and she arched toward him, wanting him to feast on her.

As she made incoherent sounds, he lifted his head, staring at her in wonder, as if he couldn't believe his luck.

She knew the feeling.

His fingers snagged the bra straps. Dragged them down. Inch by torturous inch. Until her breasts spilled out.

"Fuck me," he murmured, cupping them in his hands. "Beautiful pink..." His thumbs skimmed her nipples repeatedly until she squirmed.

When his mouth enclosed one and laved it, she almost shot off the desk. He suckled, hard, sending shards of sensation shooting straight to her clit. Making her yearn in a way she'd never dreamed possible.

"Wyatt, please..." She strained against him, needing him inside her. Now.

"Soon," he said, transferring his attentions to her other nipple while his hand insinuated its way between their bodies.

He pressed his thumb against her clit and she undulated a little, craving relief.

"Oh God, yes," she said, a second before a pounding at

the door made them jump.

"Hey sweetie, open up. Tell me what happened at the comp."

Ashlin grimaced and mouthed, "Miranda," as she contemplated ignoring her friend so she could be fucked on her desk.

But as Wyatt looked at her with a raised eyebrow, Ashlin knew the opportunity had passed.

She'd been lost in the moment, mindless with wanting Wyatt, but now that reality had intruded it would take her a while to get her head back in the game.

She needed to be swept away by lust to stop over-analyzing her failures. And sadly, that wouldn't happen in her office now with Miranda on the other side of the door.

"Sorry." She slipped her bra straps up and shrugged into her workout top, zipping it up as she headed for the door. "Raincheck?"

Wyatt winced and glanced at his groin. "Got a cold shower with my name on it around here?"

Ashlin smiled and pointed at her desk. "Take a seat behind it, she won't know what we've been up to."

After Wyatt shielded his lower half from view, Ashlin opened the door. Miranda took one look at their faces and halted.

"Uh-oh. I interrupted the horizontal shimmy, didn't I?"

Ashlin didn't risk glancing at Wyatt. Her scorching hot cheeks would spontaneously combust if she did. "Come in."

Miranda smirked and shook her head. "We can chat later."

"Stay." Wyatt stood and Ashlin knew if she glanced at his groin she'd giggle. "I just popped by to confirm you're all coming to Kurt's party tonight."

"Wouldn't miss it," Miranda said, her knowing smile

waning a little. "Though tell that Australian brother of yours if he criticizes my jewelry again I'll knee him in the balls."

Wyatt guffawed. "Fiery."

Eager to deflect Miranda's attention, Ashlin said, "Sure you haven't got a crush on Steele? Because you only fire up for the ones you like."

To her surprise, Miranda blushed. "Wyatt, your girlfriend's full of BS."

Ashlin waited for Wyatt to correct Miranda, to say she wasn't his girlfriend. Instead, he grinned, his bemused gaze swinging between the two of them.

"I'll see you both tonight," he said.

He brushed a brief kiss on Ashlin's cheek before bolting out the door, leaving her to face an inevitable interrogation, when all she felt like doing was running after Wyatt so they could finish what they'd started.

"Nice flowers." Miranda strolled into the office and touched a petal. "That guy's in love and you're just as much of a smitten kitten."

"Don't be silly." Ashlin left the door open deliberately, hoping her friend would get the hint.

Miranda pursed her lips and made mock smoochy sounds. "Considering you've never brought a guy here, let alone done him on your desk, means you're so into him."

"It's a physical thing." Ashlin shrugged, wondering if the lie sounded as hollow to Miranda. As if Wyatt accepting her labeled as his girlfriend hadn't freaked her out enough.

"Yeah, right." Her friend wolf-whistled. "Deets, please. Length? Width? Endurance?"

Ashlin made a zipping motion over her lips. "I need to head home and get ready for this party."

"Me too, honey, but we've got time." Miranda glanced at her watch and stood so fast she wobbled a little on her precarious heels. "Maybe not. I want to look ravishing tonight."

"You always do."

Miranda blew her a kiss. "Thanks, but I've never been invited to a party thrown by a star footballer. Imagine the wall to wall hotties." She fanned herself. "Not that you care, what with Wyatt being there and all."

Ashlin wished they didn't have to attend the party tonight. She'd rather be getting it on with Wyatt so she could prove to herself—and him—that the physical connection between them was all that mattered.

In fact, once they got the sexual tension out of their systems, it would prove that they had little in common beyond it. The yearning made them both a little crazy. Once they'd done the deed, she could ignore all those funny feelings inside and focus on the important stuff: getting a new job, in a new city, far from good guys whose expectations would fall far short with her.

"Sure it's the hotties you're going all out for and not Steele?"

Miranda rolled her eyes. "Puh-lease. The sooner that egotistical jerk heads back to the outback or wherever he came from, the happier I'll be."

"Protesting much?" Ashlin grinned. Oh yeah, her friend had a major crush on Wyatt's dishy Aussie brother.

Miranda muttered something derogatory in Italian under her breath as she made a beeline for the door. "I'll see you later."

Miranda raised her hand in a wave as she tottered down the corridor, in a great hurry to escape further teasing.

Tonight would be fun. Yet as Ashlin's gaze landed on the orchids, she couldn't help but wonder if she was the one protesting too much about not liking a guy.

THIRTEEN

"Who's the stunning redhead with bad taste?" Kurt elbowed Wyatt as he handed him a beer. "Appalling taste, considering the way she's been draped all over you the last fifteen minutes."

"Ashlin," Wyatt said, through gritted teeth. "And that's fifteen minutes too long that we've been here."

"Don't go getting defensive, bro." Kurt slugged him on the arm in the same way he'd done countless times growing up. Now, like then, Wyatt resisted the urge to punch him back. In the nose. "It's great seeing you so happy."

Wyatt didn't need his brother's validation but it felt good that Kurt actually noticed someone else for once. "Careful there. You're showing your metro side."

"I can be metro-sexual." Kurt winked. "The girls love it when I'm in touch with my feminine side."

Wyatt rolled his eyes. "There's always an angle with you. Anything to get some skirt."

To Wyatt's surprise, hurt replaced amusement in Kurt's gaze. "You make me sound like a heartless bastard."

Wyatt bit back the natural response, "That's because you are."

Kurt jerked his head at Ashlin. "Is it serious?"

"I want it to be." The answer tumbled from Wyatt's lips quickly, surprising them both if Kurt's comical eyebrow rising was any indication.

"Wow." Kurt's curious gaze swung between the two of them. "She doesn't look the nerdy type but hey, if you're happy, I'm happy."

Wyatt stifled a snort. Since when had Kurt's approval meant anything?

"You're full of shit," Wyatt said, relieved when he spied Steele making a beeline for them. He couldn't wait to see Kurt off-guard for once. "Here comes Steele."

Kurt stiffened, his expression cautious. "Fuck. He looks like a blond version of you."

"Lucky guy." Wyatt grinned, enjoying Kurt's discomfort and feeling a heel because of it. "So if Steele, Zane and I got the looks and the brains, what happened to you?"

"Bastard." Kurt slugged him on the arm again. "God, why does this feel so weird?"

"Because it is." Wyatt had been stunned to learn he had two Australian half-brothers yet thankfully, both Zane and Steele had been laid-back and accepting. "But we're lucky. They're good guys. Like me."

"Not a prick like me, you mean?"

Wyatt shrugged. "You said it, man."

Kurt didn't have time to respond as Steele stopped in front of them. He nodded at Wyatt, his gaze guarded as it swung to Kurt.

Neither of his older siblings spoke as they sized each other up and Wyatt felt compelled to fill the awkward silence.

"Steele, this is Kurt."

If Wyatt relegating Kurt to secondary status annoyed him, he didn't show it.

Kurt stuck out his hand. "Great to meet you."

Steele shook it. "Likewise."

But their handshake didn't last long and Wyatt wondered what would happen if he left the two alpha Harrisons alone. He'd pay to see Kurt taken down a peg or two. The golden boy hadn't had to battle for anything in his life.

"You staying in town long?" Kurt said, gripping his beer bottle tight, a sure sign he was rattled.

"Another few weeks." Steele pointed to where Zane chatted with Chantal. "Wanted to catch up with the little guy, make sure he was staying out of trouble."

Their chuckles didn't sound forced. Zane towered over Steele by a good four inches.

"Don't blame you," Kurt said, smirking. "We need to make sure our younger bros behave."

"Like I'm the one prone to trouble," Wyatt muttered, somewhat buoyed to see Kurt and Steele exchange conspiratorial big-brother grins. "The only reason you haven't been locked up is because people revere bozos who play football."

Kurt's mock outrage as he flipped his middle finger made Steele laugh.

"Yeah, what's with that, Wyatt?" Steele said. "I make the tough decisions, Zane's toughest decision is what sneakers to wear to training, and people fall at his feet?"

"Beats me," Wyatt said, pleased it was his turn to side with Steele. "Speaking of Zane, let's get him over here..." Wyatt trailed off, horrified when he glimpsed Christopher striding into the room.

"What's wrong?" Steele glanced over his shoulder and froze.

Furious, Wyatt turned to Kurt. "I told you not to invite him."

"I didn't." Kurt appeared suitably surprised but Wyatt had no idea if he faked it. "Since when has Dad not done exactly as he pleased?"

"Asshole," Wyatt muttered, not sure if he referred to his father or brother. "Come on, Steele, let's go join the ladies."

Kurt held up his hands. "Hey, look, I'm sorry."

"You've got nothing to apologize for." Steele's flinty gaze made Wyatt want to rub his arms it was that cold. "Unlike that old bastard." He nodded at Kurt. "Good meeting you, but I'm not hanging around to confront him here."

"Understood." Kurt hesitated a second before slinging an arm over their shoulders. "I want us to be friends so let's all have dinner before I fly back to LA, okay?"

Touched by his brother's rare show of emotion, Wyatt nodded. "Okay. We'll catch you later."

Leaving Kurt to deal with Christopher, Wyatt fell into step with Steele, all but running for the opposite end of the massive ballroom Kurt had hired for the party.

"Can't believe he had the gall to show up here," Steele muttered, fury making his words sound forced and staccato. "Gutless bastard. Probably thought confronting me in front of a room full of people would make our first meeting in thirty-three years easier."

"That's his MO," Wyatt said. "Taking the easy way out."

Steele's jaw clenched tight, making his neck muscles stand out, before he blew out a long breath. "Zane never should've opened the door to any kind of contact with him."

"You can't blame him for wanting a relationship with his father."

Wyatt should know. He'd craved it growing up, until finally realizing at graduation that nothing he said or did or achieved would make a mark with his narcissistic father.

"No, I guess not." Steele huffed out a breath. "It's just seeing him again, after all this time..." He rubbed at his chest. "Didn't think he had the power to affect me anymore but he has."

Wishing they knew each other well enough for Wyatt to give Steele a bear hug, he settled for a hand on the shoulder. "Don't sweat it. We all deal with stuff in our own way."

"Thanks, mate." Steele took a few deep breaths and straightened. "But I need to get out of here."

"Sure, let me say bye to Ashlin and I'll come with you."

"You don't have to do that."

"I want to." Wyatt shrugged, Steele's palpable gratefulness making his throat tighten. "We're brothers. We need to stick together."

Steele glanced away and blinked. Wyatt knew the feeling.

He'd never cried, even as a kid. Tears were wasted. Emotions futile. Kurt had been the one to throw tantrums to get his way. It had worked. Their mom had doted on her eldest and Christopher thought the sun shone out of his ass. Wyatt had learned early in life that being quiet and introspective served him better. Avoid conflict. Do his own thing. Fuck the world.

But as he reached Ashlin and she smiled at him with warmth and admiration, he knew he'd met the one person to rock his previously staid, stable, comfortable world.

"What's wrong?" She touched his arm. "You look shell-shocked."

"Christopher has shown up uninvited," he said, his voice

low. "Steele can't hang around so is it okay if I leave with him and come back for you later?"

"Sure." She kissed his cheek, making him feel ten foot tall. "I'll try to stay away from the hot footballers in the meantime."

"I won't." Miranda piped up, not ashamed to be eavesdropping. "My eyes are hurting with all this candy on show."

Steele sniggered, masking it behind a cough when Miranda glared.

"Uh-oh," Ashlin murmured. "Miranda's got this thing for your brother and it's making her a little crazy."

"Gotcha. We'll make our escape now," he said. "Steele, let's hit the road—"

"What's your problem?" Miranda eyeballed Steele, almost standing toe to toe with him. "You don't want to stick around and party so don't judge those of us who do."

"Hey, I didn't say a word." Steele held up his hands in surrender, a smirk tugging at his mouth.

"You didn't have to." Miranda pointed at his face. "That smug expression says it all."

Wyatt glanced at Ashlin, who was smiling, enjoying the show as much as him.

Steele shrugged. "Maybe I've got something to be smug about?"

"Like what?" Miranda frowned; it did little to detract from the brunette's beauty. She might be small and feisty, but Wyatt guessed she'd have guys falling at her feet.

By his brother's mutinous expression, Steele wouldn't be one of them.

Steele leaned in close. "Wouldn't you like to know?"

To Wyatt's surprise, Miranda blushed. With her fieriness, he didn't expect her to embarrass easily.

"I think you're all talk." Miranda folded her arms, giving

her cleavage a nice boost in the process. And by Steele's sharp intake of breath, he'd noticed.

"And I think you're full of it, but hey, I'm not going to hold that against you," Steele said, doffing an imaginary cap. "Now if you'll excuse me, my lady, I've got more important things to do than trade meaningless banter."

Miranda puffed up like an outraged bullfrog. "You rude assho—"

"Come on, Miranda, there's a cocktail over there with our name on it," Ashlin said, dragging Miranda away, mouthing 'sorry' to Steele and Wyatt over her shoulder.

"See you soon, *sweetheart*," Steele called out to Miranda's retreating back.

Miranda flipped him the bird without looking back.

"What is it with you two?" Wyatt pointed at Miranda. "You barely know each other yet you carry on like an old married couple."

"She's got the hots for me." A bashful grin stole across Steele's face. "What's a guy to do?"

Wyatt laughed. "Come on. Let's go get a beer."

They'd made it as far as the door when Christopher stepped in front of them, effectively barring their exit.

"Hey, Son."

Wyatt felt his jaw almost hit the floor. Christopher never called him 'Son'. Ever. The fact he did it for the first time in front of Steele, his firstborn? Huge gaff. Massive.

"Christopher." Wyatt managed a curt nod, not daring to glance at Steele, considering he could feel the tension radiating off him. "Kurt said you weren't invited so what are you doing here?"

"I came to see my sons. All of them." Christopher wasn't looking at him, his somber gaze fixed on Steele. "Good to see you, Son."

"Don't you dare call me that," Steele said, his tone a low hiss as he stepped forward, in Christopher's face. "Don't you fucking dare."

Taken aback, Christopher glanced at Wyatt for help. Yeah, like that would happen.

Christopher refocused on Steele and cleared his throat. "Look, Son, I'm sorry—"

"Stick your lousy apology up your arse." Steele leaned in even closer, his nose almost touching Christopher's. "You've had years to apologize to me and Zane. Yet you choose our first meeting to be at a fucking party?" He sneered, tension making his body vibrate. "You have no right to call me your son and you never will. So don't come near me again. Got it?"

Steele shoved passed a gaping Christopher and half jogged down the hall leading to the ballroom's foyer.

"You shouldn't have come," Wyatt said, almost feeling sorry for his father. Almost. "Steele's right. This wasn't the time or place."

"I needed to see him." Christopher blinked rapidly, his voice a husky croak. "It's been so long..."

"Why is that?" Wyatt quashed his momentary sympathy. Christopher was a master manipulator and his current show of emotion could be just that: a show.

"I made a mistake." Christopher gazed at Steele, a blip in the distance as he pushed through the building's front double doors.

"Which you've had years to rectify."

Christopher's gaze swung back to him, accusatory. "Why do you always do that? Make me out to be the bad guy."

"Maybe because you are," Wyatt said, disappointed that even now, his father couldn't take responsibility for the dog act of abandoning his first two sons. "The thing is, you left your family behind to start a new one. And you weren't much chop with our family either. That makes you a deadbeat dad."

Christopher's brows drew together. "You little punk—"

"Yeah, that's me. The punk who's a self-made millionaire by using initiative and brains. The punk whose Aussie brothers are happy to hang around with. The punk who never lived up to your expectations because I couldn't throw a football like your golden boy Kurt."

Unaware his voice had risen, Wyatt lowered it when a waiter glanced their way. "The punk who has some advice for you. If you want Steele and Zane to have anything to do with you, you better be a damned better father to them than you were to me."

With that, Wyatt headed in the same direction as Steele.

He'd wanted to say that shit to his father for years and it should feel good to get it off his chest. It didn't. Instead, tears stung his eyes and he dashed his hand across them, determined not to cry over Christopher.

He'd learned the hard way his father wasn't worth it.

FOURTEEN

Ashlin saw the confrontation between Christopher Harrison and his sons, Wyatt and Steele, from twenty feet away. It didn't look pretty. And the devastation on Wyatt's face as he left made her chest ache in a way she knew wouldn't be soothed by partying with Miranda.

She needed to go after him.

"Sweetie, I have to go." She pecked Miranda's cheek. "You going to be okay?"

Thankfully, Miranda's bluster over Steele had petered out once she'd slurped half a Mojito. There were some major sparks between those two and Ashlin couldn't wait to see what developed while the commanding Aussie stayed in town for the next few weeks.

Miranda raised her cocktail glass. "Sure. I see a footballer over there with my name tattooed on his forehead."

"Have fun." Ashlin gave her a gentle nudge in the direction of the footballer. "Fill me in on the details tomorrow."

Miranda had already wandered off, leaving Ashlin to dodge dancing partygoers on the parquetry floor as she headed after Wyatt. As she reached the ballroom exit, she spied him leaving the building, and picked up the pace.

When her cell, tucked into the pocket of her slim-line leather jacket, vibrated against her hip, she ignored it. Until she remembered the email she'd received earlier, from a premier dance company in the UK, ascertaining her interest in the lead choreographer position for their upcoming season.

Her steps faltered as she dug the cell out of her pocket, glanced at the screen and recognized an international number.

Damn, she had to take this.

Hitting the call answer button with her thumb, she took a deep breath and raised the phone to her ear.

"Ashlin O'Meara speaking."

"Just the woman I wanted to speak to." The clipped English accent made her pulse race. This could be it. The job offer of a lifetime. "Graham Thorpesman here. Did you receive our email, Miss O'Meara? Because we heard about your competition win and we're very keen to have you onboard."

She'd done it. Landed the best job of her career. So why the dithering?

"Thanks for the offer, I'm thrilled." Then why the shaky hands and slight quiver in her voice? Damn it.

"So that's an acceptance?"

Ashlin hesitated. She wanted to yell 'hell yeah'. But a small part of her felt disloyal somehow, like she should be discussing this with Wyatt.

Crazy, considering they weren't in a long-term relationship and she'd known a new job in a new place would be a real possibility when they'd started up. She'd even told him how stagnant her life in Vegas was and that she craved a change. But now that her dreams had become a reality, she couldn't help but feel confused.

Wyatt was a good guy. One of the best. And she'd grown used to having him around, even for a few weeks. She'd miss him. Miss *them*. But that didn't mean she'd give up the opportunity of a lifetime.

Taking a deep breath, she steadied her resolve. "Thanks for the offer. I'd love to be your lead choreographer."

"Excellent. You start in two weeks," Graham said. "We'll email you a formal job offer with conditions and remuneration within the hour. Glad to have you onboard."

"Thank you." Ashlin hung up, her hands shaking as she slipped the cell back into her pocket.

She'd reached the pinnacle of her career. Landed the kind of job that would garner worldwide recognition and guarantee her a walk-in role at any premier dance company on the planet.

Yet as she jogged toward the front doors, hoping she could still catch Wyatt, all she could think was 'how am I going to tell him?'

FIFTEEN

Wyatt paced his hotel suite, at a loss. Steele hadn't wanted to talk after their run-in with Christopher and Wyatt didn't know his half-brother well enough to push the issue.

Steele had looked shell-shocked when they'd got back to the hotel, a guy operating on autopilot. He'd ignored Wyatt's overtures for conversation, answering in monosyllabic grunts. So Wyatt had taken the hint and left him the hell alone.

Wyatt didn't blame him for needing time to assimilate what had happened. Their father had confronted Steele for the first time in decades. God, he could barely handle Christopher's impromptu appearance and he'd lived with the guy for eighteen years before moving out.

He couldn't imagine how Steele must be feeling and was suitably outraged on his behalf. Enough to want to kick something. So he did. A table leg. It didn't help. Anger and frustration and helplessness rolled through him and damn, he needed an outlet.

A light knock sounded at the door and he strode toward it, hoping Steele had changed his mind. Maybe they could play a round of racquetball to burn off this unsettling feeling. No talk. Just action.

However, when he opened the door, Ashlin stood there, gnawing her bottom lip, uncertainty clouding her eyes.

Whereas for the first time in a long time, he'd never been more certain of anything.

"You okay?" she said, slipping past him.

He shut the door and spun around, snagging her arm. "I am now."

She must've heard something in his voice. A hint of desperation. Frustration.

Whatever it was, her eyebrow raised slowly and the corners of her mouth followed suit. "Anything I can do?"

"This." He hauled her into his arms, backed her against the wall and slammed his mouth on hers.

He needed this. Needed *her*. Craved her with an intensity that scared the shit out of him, the type of yearning where he'd never wanted anything so badly in his entire life.

Ashlin could fill the void.

Beautiful. Sweet. Heart-rending. Ashlin.

She moaned deep in her throat, her body plastered to his. He was rock hard. Needed to be inside her. Wanted to make her come for him. Only him.

He wrenched his mouth from hers. "You make me crazy with wanting you."

"Feeling's mutual," she said, tracing his mouth with a fingertip, her gaze filled with so much emotion it made him choke up. "I need to tell you—"

"I know," he said, pressing a finger to her lips. "I feel it too. In here." He pressed her palm against his chest, over his heart. "I know I said this was a short term thing but I like you and now I think I'm falling harder and I'm fucking terrified and—"

This time she kissed him. Silencing his babbling. Preventing him from making more of a fool of himself than he already had.

And she kept on kissing him while undoing his belt buckle. Snapping the top button on his jeans. Unzipping him. When she slid her hand inside his jocks, wrapped her fingers around his cock and squeezed, he was pretty damn sure he'd died and gone to heaven.

But this time, he wasn't doing this without ensuring her pleasure first.

He stilled her hand and gently withdrew it from his fly.

"It's your turn," he murmured against the side of her mouth, raining tiny kisses across her jaw to her ear. "Let me love you."

Fuck. He meant make love, but somehow the L word had slipped out and now it hung there in the silence, punctuated by their heavy breathing.

Would she freak out? Because he sure as hell was. For a guy who didn't do emotions, no way did he do love.

But rather than push him away as he half expected, she smiled, radiating a joy he'd never seen before. She took his hand and led him to the bed in the far corner of the suite. With a soft shove, she pushed him onto the bed.

"Don't move. Just watch," she murmured.

So he did. Watched as she untied the knot of her halter dress and let it fall to her waist, baring her breasts. Watched as she shimmied out of the dress, letting it pool at her feet. Watched as she pushed white lace panties down her long legs, leaving her gloriously, eye-poppingly naked.

He stared at the golden-red landing strip between her legs. Aching to be there.

"I want you," she said, her voice barely above a whisper. "But I'm scared I'll disappoint you—"

"Don't." He surged upward, placed his hands around her waist and drew her closer. "You could never do that."

With her crotch at face level, he leaned forward and tongued her, relieved when she jolted. He teased her clit with his tongue. Lapping at it. Circling it. Nipping it. Buoyed when her legs wobbled. Encouraged as she dug her fingers into his scalp.

He toyed with her slick folds. Slipped one finger inside her. Another. Withdrew and pushed inside repeatedly, alternating with laving her clit until her rapid breathing and muted moans filled the air.

She was close. So close. But he had no idea if she'd reached this point before and been unable to go all the way. She must be feeling pretty damn vulnerable right now and he had to show her he felt the same way. So he paused for a moment and glanced up.

"I love you," he said, searching for some sign he hadn't ruined this before it had begun.

He didn't need to hear it in return. He didn't need some hollow declaration she didn't mean. But he hoped she knew how much it cost him, a guy who hadn't loved a woman before, to say it.

"Right back at you," she said, arching her hips toward him. "Now keep going and let me show you how much."

Happier than he'd ever been, he said, "You're close?"

"You have no idea how close..."

He tongued her again, quickly escalating the pace until her hips ground against his mouth. Anchoring her ass with his hands, he licked and licked until she tensed, a second before she shattered on a scream that made him feel ten feet tall.

She sagged against him and he eased her down onto the

bed until they lay side by side, facing each other. Nowhere to hide.

He'd expected to feel a fool, verbalizing how he felt. Instead, as she stared at him like he'd performed a minor miracle, he knew he'd done the right thing.

He just knew it.

ASHLIN'S BODY throbbed with the intensity of her orgasm. Her first in a long, *loooong* time. Not since Dougal had she experienced the bone-melting aftershocks, and even then it hadn't been as good as this.

Wyatt was a master. A sex-god.

But she knew it was more than that.

The moment he'd revealed his feelings and told her he loved her, she'd let go and opened herself up to the possibility of pleasure again.

She'd been carrying guilt around for a long time, had known it hampered her emotionally, but it wasn't until she'd seen the love in Wyatt's eyes had she realized it had been affecting her physically too.

The reason she hadn't been able to orgasm all these years was because she believed she didn't deserve pleasure.

She'd always known it deep down, in that secret place filled with self-loathing and self-recrimination after the choice she'd made.

She hadn't deserved to feel good, not after what she'd done.

She'd known it had been a life-altering decision at the time. Heck, it had ruined her relationship with Dougal and made him run. But the fallout from her choice had infiltrated every aspect of her life and she hadn't realized how much until Wyatt had accepted her.

But would he feel the same way if he knew what she'd done?

He hadn't noticed the small scars that bore testament to the life-changing decision all those years ago in London. She almost wished he had noticed before he'd given her that earth-shattering orgasm; wished he'd asked about it, so she could've finally told him the truth. Because after what he'd just done and what he'd said? It would make telling him all the harder.

Wyatt was perfect. The most genuine, caring, sweet guy she'd ever known. Which pretty much solidified her decision.

She had to leave ASAP.

She was flawed and would fall short against Wyatt's perfection. Would always fall short of his high expectations. No, better to leave now, before that love in his eyes turned to hate.

She'd seen it happen before.

But first, she had to have one momentous memory to sustain her through a cold London winter.

"Condom?" She rested her hand against his chest, caressing his pecs, his abs.

"Top drawer," he said, staring at her like he couldn't quite believe they were actually doing this. "Are we going to mention the fact you came?"

"No need." She grabbed a condom, ripped the foil packet and reached for him. "I think this entire floor of the hotel had that fact confirmed."

He laughed, but it faded fast. "Seriously, sweetheart, was it good?"

"The best." She brushed her lips across his as she rolled the condom on. "Thank you."

"My pleasure." His proud grin made her chuckle. "In

case you were wondering, there's plenty more where that came from."

A sharp pain stabbed at her chest. Sadly, there wouldn't be, so she had to make every second count now.

"You talk too much." She straddled him, pinning his shoulders to the bed, delighting in his tortured yet rapturous expression as she eased down onto him, inch by exquisite inch.

He felt amazing inside her. Filling her. The right thickness. The right length. Like he was made for her.

But as he gripped her hips and thrust upward, withdrawing and doing it again and again and again until they were both mindless with passion, she knew that wasn't possible.

Good guys like Wyatt weren't made for bad girls like her.

So she took what she could. Riding him until the pleasure consumed her. Consumed him. And as she lay collapsed on his chest, cradled in the security of his arms, she knew what she had to do. The problem was, how could she do it, when it would break both their hearts?

Trying to ignore the ache spreading through her chest, she rolled off him and scuttled to the edge of the bed.

"Hey. Where do you think you're going?"

"Home," she said, clearing her throat when her response sounded like a mouse on helium. "I need to start packing."

The bed shifted and she stood, not wanting him to reach for her, touch her, not now. She couldn't bear it.

"What's wrong?" The warmth had leeched from his voice, replaced by the circumspection he'd sported when they'd first met.

She didn't blame him. He had every right to be

mistrustful of her, considering she was about to drive a stake through his heart.

Quickly re-dressing, she inhaled a deep breath and turned to face him. Bad move. The ache in her chest turned into a sharp, stabbing pain as she saw his big brown eyes filled with solemnity, his dark rumpled curls, his tanned torso, highlighted by the crisp whiteness of his sheets. He looked oddly vulnerable, half tucked in bed, and she belatedly wished she'd waited until they were both dressed to do this.

"I've been offered an amazing job in London."

"Congratulations." He sat up straighter and the damn sheet covering his lower half slipped. "What are you going to do?"

"I've accepted it and leave in three days." A small white lie but she needed to end this here and now. Now that they'd declared their feelings, no point in dragging this out. Better to end this relationship now before she hurt him any more.

"But...I mean, I knew this was coming...what about us..." He shook his head, confusion contorting his brow. "So that's it? We don't talk about what this new job means for us? We end this before it's really begun?"

Tears burned the back of her eyes as she nodded. "We both knew going into this it had a limited time frame. I'm over Vegas. Time to move on."

His lips compressed in a thin, stubborn line, his glare mutinous. "But that was before...fuck, we just said we loved each other."

Ashlin couldn't take this anymore. She couldn't hash this out. She'd tried once before to convince a guy what was best for both of them. It hadn't worked back then and she couldn't bear to go through it again. It would kill her.

So she reached for the most hurtful, hateful lie she could think of to end things with Wyatt once and for all.

"A woman will say anything for her first orgasm in years." She forced a smirk, while something inside her broke. "This has been fun while it lasted, so thanks."

She made a run for the door, his angry, incredulous 'what the fuck' doing little to eradicate her final memory of Wyatt: the desolation twisting his face into an expression akin to grief.

She'd done that to him.

And she'd never forgive herself for it.

SIXTEEN

Wyatt slouched on the couch in his hotel room, wearing two-day-old running shorts and surrounded by empty minibar bottles. He'd already called room service twice tonight to replenish supplies but they'd ignored his third call so maybe he'd been cut off. Fuck them. He'd get dressed and go out to continue drinking himself into oblivion.

But as he sat forward and his head moved, the memories crashed over him anew and he sank back with a groan.

He'd survived the last ten days by focusing on work all day and drinking all night. He'd had minimal interaction with anyone, citing off-site testing, to avoid going to Burlesque Bombshells the first few days when there'd been a chance of running into Ashlin.

Ashlin.

Fuck, she'd ripped out his heart, trampled it and tossed it away.

How the hell had he got it so wrong?

He'd put himself out there for the first time ever. Had let himself fall for her. Had fucking *told* her.

And she'd left without a backward glance.

He was such a chump. All she'd wanted was to get off and once he'd done that for her, she'd bolted. To the other side of the world.

He pressed his fingertips into his temples, knowing it would do little to stave off the blinder of a headache threatening to squeeze his skull. It wasn't the alcohol as much as thoughts of Ashlin and how meaningless she'd considered their relationship that caused it.

A knock sounded at the door. He ignored it for a moment, until he realized it could be Room Service taking pity on him and ready to replenish the minibar.

He padded across the room, not caring that he staggered a little. The faster he reached oblivion tonight the better. However, when he opened the door, it wasn't a hotel employee that greeted him.

Glaring at his brothers, he growled. "Who the fuck are you, the three musketeers?"

Zane grinned, Steele frowned and Kurt pushed his way into the room. "Get dressed, bozo."

"What the hell for?"

"Because I don't want to have to kick your sorry ass in those stinking shorts." Kurt shoved him toward the bathroom. "Go shower. Dress. And get back here in five minutes."

"Bully," Wyatt muttered, eyeballing Zane and Steele. "What are you all doing here?"

"Consider this an intervention," Steele said, his resolute tone brooking no argument. "We're done watching you wallow and we're not leaving here without you."

Zane nodded. "It's what brothers do. Stick together in the tough times."

Wyatt made a run for the bathroom, before the tears stinging his eyes spilled over and he made an ass of himself.

Kurt had never stood by him for anything, but he'd taken time out of his busy schedule to fly here, probably on the urging of his Aussie half-siblings, and it spoke volumes.

As for Zane and Steele, the fact they cared enough about him to be here now meant more than they'd ever know.

He may be a sorry-ass in love but he'd sure lucked in with his siblings.

A shower and a shave helped him sober up and a few minutes later he sauntered out of the bathroom to find his suite cleared of empty bottles and three pairs of accusing eyes.

Sheepish, he chose a seat opposite his brothers. If he had to face an inquisition, best to get it over with. "Before you say anything, I'm fine and while I appreciate the visit—"

"Shut the hell up," Kurt said, folding his arms. "We're here to help."

"I don't need your help—"

To Wyatt's surprise, Kurt seemed to deflate before his eyes, his big, broad shoulders slumping. "I know I've been a lousy brother. But seeing how close these two are" —he jerked a thumb in Zane and Steele's direction— "and how much they care about you in a short space of time, makes me feel like a real shit." He fidgeted with his shirt cuffs, oddly defenseless in a way Wyatt had never seen. "I'm sorry for being a self-absorbed prick all these years. I'll try to do better."

Wyatt blinked. Squeezed his eyes shut and opened them. "Who are you and what the hell have you done with my brother?"

Kurt's rueful smile made Wyatt want to hug him.

"Blame these two bozos. They must breed them super soft down under."

"Fuck you," Steele said, no spite in his comeback.

"Is it too soon for a group hug?" Zane said and they all chuckled.

Wyatt wished the ache in his chest would ease. "Seriously, guys, I appreciate you checking in on me but I'm doing okay—"

"Bullshit," Steele said, taking over from Kurt. More surprising, Kurt let him, which convinced Wyatt his brother was serious about turning over a new leaf. "You're either holed up at Bombshells working or hiding out here, drinking yourself into a stupor if the number of bottles we cleared away were any indication."

Steele crossed his arms, his body language so much like Kurt that the pain in Wyatt's chest amplified. "What's going on? Is this about the redhead?"

Wyatt didn't want to talk about Ashlin. He didn't want to divulge to his three super stud brothers that he was a grade A loser with women. So he lied.

"Ashlin and I agreed on a short term fling, so that's that. But a major freelance job fell through so I've potentially lost a shitload of money."

His brothers frowned collectively.

"Are you in financial strife?" Kurt sat forward, bracing his elbows on his knees. "Because I can help you out, just say the word."

Feeling a heel for lying, Wyatt shook his head. "Thanks, but I'm good. Just shook my confidence, you know?"

"Yeah, I know." Kurt winced and pointed at his right knee. "Been having a bit of trouble with this and the docs are talking surgery, so I'm not feeling as invincible as usual."

Wyatt gaped. Kurt admitting any weakness was like

discovering an un-hackable computer: completely mind-blowing.

"Snap," Zane said. "When my knee blew and I had a reconstruction, took me ages to heal up here." He tapped his head. "But it was a blessing in disguise, considering it made me re-evaluate a lot of shit and I ended up here." He grinned, and Wyatt envied his half-sibling's eternal optimism. "Come on, guys, you know you want that group hug real bad."

"You're an idiot," Steele said, mock-wrestling Zane until he yelled 'truce'.

Kurt cleared his throat and glanced away. Wyatt knew the feeling. Seeing Zane and Steele's closeness made his throat tighten too, but considering Kurt cared enough to be here meant there was hope for them too.

After a quick swipe at his eyes, Kurt stood. "Come on, bozos, enough of the mushy shit. Let's hit that cocktail party."

"What cocktail party..." Realization dawned. Tonight was the monthly party Chantal threw for her employees at Burlesque Bombshells. Which meant it had been four weeks since Ashlin had bowled up to him at that party and turned his world upside down.

No way in hell did he need to stroll down that particular memory lane.

Zane stood. "We're not leaving here without you."

Steele nodded, standing between Zane and Kurt to form an intimidating line. "So you do this the easy way and come with us, or we drag you with us anyway."

"You're all frigging bullies," Wyatt muttered. "I'm not a party guy—"

"Stay an hour. For us?" Zane's pleading expression could've convinced a nun to dance burlesque.

"You're pathetic," Wyatt said, but he knew he was beaten. "One hour tops, okay?"

"Done." Kurt slapped him on the back. "Come on, bro. Let's go bond some more."

For once, Wyatt didn't have a smart-ass comeback for his brother.

SEVENTEEN

"You all packed?" Miranda lounged on the sole chair in Ashlin's bedroom, totally rocking a strapless red satin sheath that ended above her knees.

"Yeah." Ashlin zipped her last suitcase and plopped on the bed beside it. "Thanks for the help, by the way. Not."

Miranda laughed and gestured at her outfit. "Couldn't risk a zip snagging this." She held her hands at length, studying her nails. "Or ruining this manicure."

Ashlin stared at Miranda's crimson nails. "Since when do you get your nails painted anything other than clear?"

"Since I need to make a point." Miranda stood and cocked a hip. "I have to make that supercilious idiot weep at the cocktail party tonight."

Ashlin snickered. "You've still got a thing for Steele?"

"I don't have anything but a distinct dislike for that jerk," Miranda said, making a mockery of her statement when she blushed. "He rubs me up the wrong way."

"Don't forget he's transient and it may not be worth starting up if you really like him," Ashlin said, wishing she'd had the wisdom to take her own advice.

Miranda nudged a suitcase aside and sat next to her. "Is that why you ended things with Wyatt? Because you're moving to London?"

Ashlin's heart ached as it always did when she thought of Wyatt; too often. "It's more complicated than that."

"Life's complicated, honey." Miranda studied her, tiny worry lines between her immaculately waxed brows. "If he's worth it, you work it out."

Wyatt was so worth it but Ashlin wasn't, that was the problem.

"Look, you've had me feed you Intel all week so you wouldn't run into him at Bombshells, so it must be pretty intense between you two if you wanted to avoid him that bad." Miranda patted her knee. "Whatever it is, I've never seen you back down from a challenge, so why don't you give it a go? Long distance can work."

"The distance isn't the problem." It's what she'd done the last time she'd been in London that ensured she could never be with Wyatt beyond short-term. "I've done some stuff in my past."

Miranda squeezed her knee and let go. "We all have."

"Yeah? What's the perfect girl done in her past that's so bad?" Considering Miranda's clean living, hippy lifestyle, Ashlin couldn't imagine her doing anything worse than littering. "Served up store-bought pasta rather than homemade? Missed Mass two Sundays in a row?" Ashlin covered her mouth in mock horror. "Maybe slept with a boy so you're not a virgin on your wedding night?"

She'd expected Miranda to laugh. She hadn't expected her eyes to fill with tears.

"Shit, sweetie, I'm sorry. I was joking." Ashlin hugged her friend. "You okay?"

Miranda sniffled then nodded. "Everyone's got a past.

Trust me on that. So whatever you did, whatever you can't forget, get a grip on it and move on."

Ashlin wished she could. But not living up to Dougal's expectations had ruined her for years. Not living up to Wyatt's expectations would destroy her completely.

"Running from the past doesn't change anything." Miranda gripped her shoulders and gave her a little shake. "I made a stand and here I am today. When are you going to make your stand and confront whatever's putting that haunted look in your eyes?"

Haunted? Was it that obvious?

Miranda's grip tightened. "Honey, Chantal and I know something's been bugging you for as long as we've known you. But we've never pushed because we love you. And like I said, we've all got baggage. Hell, I've got a full airport's worth." Miranda pulled her in for a quick hug before releasing her. "But if it affects you to the point you look perpetually sad? You've got to do something about it." Miranda pressed a hand to her heart. "Trust me, I know. Boy, do I know."

Ashlin quelled her curiosity. She had no right to ask about Miranda's past when she had no intention of divulging her own.

Only one person deserved to hear about what she'd done and thanks to her friend's pep talk, she may just tell him.

She owed him that much after all he'd done for her.

Wyatt had made her feel alive for the first time in years. He'd broken through her barriers and made her *feel*. In a way she'd never thought she could again.

She loved him. And he'd been the one to open her up to the possibility of loving again.

Yeah, she owed him.

Telling him the truth would be the least she could do after the way she'd treated him. And then she could leave, knowing she'd done her best to make things right despite doing everything so wrong.

"Thanks, sweetie, you're the best." Ashlin hugged Miranda.

"And don't you forget it." Miranda dabbed at the corners of her eyes with her pinkies. "Now go sort things out with your hot man."

Ashlin didn't need to be told twice.

EIGHTEEN

Wyatt stayed true to his word. He stuck around for an hour at the cocktail party, with Zane, Steele and Kurt hovering over him.

They'd plied him with sodas between the occasional beer, monitoring his alcohol intake like the frigging police. They'd made sure he ate his body weight in smoked chicken wings and curly fries. They'd told tall tales to make him laugh. They'd miraculously stayed clear of the beautiful women buzzing around. Even Zane, who couldn't resist the occasional glance in Chantal's direction, stuck to his side.

Wyatt should've felt smothered. He didn't. For a guy who didn't believe in emotional attachments he'd sure turned into a sentimental schmuck.

He appreciated the effort his brothers had gone to in getting him to man up. If they hadn't, he'd still be moping around his hotel suite. At least this way, he could ditch them with a clear conscience and go finish up some work before he wrapped up this job tomorrow.

"Thanks guys, but I'm outta here." He tapped his watch.

"I've hung around for sixty minutes on the dot and now I've got some work I want to finish."

Kurt slugged him on the arm. "You're a sad case."

"But we kinda like you anyway." Steele punched his other arm. "If anyone can understand the urge to finish off business before midnight, I do, so you're off the hook."

Zane nodded. "But if you need us, we're here for the next few hours, okay?"

"Thanks," Wyatt said, grateful for his brothers and the way they'd rallied around him when he'd needed them most. "For everything."

Kurt rolled his eyes. "Fuck, let him go before he drags us all down with the mushy shit."

They laughed and as Wyatt walked away he felt lighter than he had in years.

He'd closed himself off from any kind of in-depth human contact for a long time and letting his brothers in made him feel whole.

While he didn't need a mood spoiler right now, he couldn't help but wonder if there was hope for his father. If Kurt could change, maybe Christopher could too?

He couldn't see it happening but considering the lengths Zane had gone to, travelling to the US to meet the family he'd never known, maybe Wyatt could make an overture toward his father? Pave the way for Zane and Steele?

His father was a cocky, blustering bastard, but maybe he was all front? Kurt had a similar brash personality and maybe that's why they'd gotten on so well, while Wyatt had deliberately erected barriers because he felt inferior somehow?

Whatever made his father behave like a callous prick, now wasn't the time. He'd consider reaching out to Christopher when he felt less vulnerable. Being metaphorically kicked in the balls by the woman he loved wasn't conducive to building emotional bridges with his aloof father.

Thankfully, the guys hadn't brought up the subject of Ashlin again. Either Chantal had warned Zane not to mention it, and he'd told Steele and Kurt, or his brothers had bought his lie about the freelance job falling through and accepted his short-term fling excuse.

Regardless, he needed to get this work done and put Bombshells, and Ashlin, behind him.

However, that seemed impossible as he entered Chantal's office and came face to face with the woman he couldn't forget no matter how hard he tried.

"What the hell are you doing here?" He inadvertently slammed the door, shock making his hand shake as he rubbed it over his face. Maybe he hadn't sobered up as much as he'd thought and he'd conjured her up out of thin air. "I thought you left for London last week?"

She shook her head, her glorious red hair tumbling over her shoulders and making his fingers itch to touch it. "I've been around, avoiding you."

Bile rose in his throat and he swallowed it. What had he done wrong for her to hate him this much? Love really was for suckers.

"So what's this? An aberration?" He sneered, anger making his gut clench. "Because I've got work to do and I'd appreciate you leaving me the hell alone so I can get on with it."

She blinked rapidly, as if trying to stave off the animosity that rolled off him in waves. "Not before I tell you the truth."

"Didn't you do that already?" He snapped his fingers. "About how you used me to get off, then lied about loving me, and accepted a job overseas without considering a long distance relationship?" He pretended to stagger a little. "The truth hurts, babe, but I'm over it. Over you." He spat the last two words, injecting enough venom to make her flinch.

She nodded, slowly, like her neck hurt. "I'm glad, because it'll make this easier."

She perched on the edge of his desk, oblivious when she nudged several USBs and they tumbled to the floor. "I lied to you. Pushed you away deliberately. Because you're too good for me and ultimately that would've ended things between us."

"What the fuck?" Incredulous, he gaped, before snapping his jaw shut. "I'm too *good* for you? Are you for real?"

"Let me explain." She took a deep breath and he silently cursed himself for staring at her boobs and remembering how they felt in his hands.

"I'm fickle. I ran away from my family in Ireland when I was eighteen and they basically disowned me. They wanted me to study teaching at university, I wanted to dance."

So far she hadn't told him anything he didn't already know and he was tempted to turn around and head out the door without looking back.

"So I went to London, met Dougal, fell in love," she huffed out a long breath, "and got pregnant."

That captured his attention. "You had a kid?"

Her mouth compressed with sorrow. "I had an abortion."

Shit. She'd gone through a lot as a teen.

"Not because I was too young, but because it would've interfered with my dreams of being a top dancer. Plus having an illegitimate child would've proved my family right, that I wasn't prepared to take on the world." She said it defiantly, like she expected him to judge her, but he remained silent. "According to Dougal, I was a selfish, heartless bitch and he left me."

She pressed her fingers into her eyes before lowering them. "The irony was, I had complications that mucked me up pretty bad internally and the time I had off ensured I missed out on my dream job as a dancer. So I danced small parts through Europe, ended up in Paris, fell in love with burlesque and became a choreographer instead."

Wyatt could understand why she had self-esteem issues, believing he was better than her, but it still didn't explain the rest. "Are you expecting me to judge you? Is that why you said all that bullshit about me being too good for you?"

Her eyebrows rose, as she absentmindedly wrung her hands. "You seriously don't think I'm selfish for what I did?"

He shrugged. "You were young. Naive. And you did what was right for you at the time. No one has the right to judge you on a decision you made back then."

That's when it hit him, the reason for her inability to achieve physical satisfaction. "Is that why you couldn't come all these years? You've been beating yourself up over it, because you feel guilty and undeserving?"

She bit her bottom lip, nodded. "I figured that out after the last time we...when you said you loved me...guess I felt deserving in that moment and I let myself go..."

He wanted to go to her then. Wanted to bundle her into his arms and soothe her and make it all better. But he'd already hung himself out to dry once with her and he'd be damned if he did it again.

"Why didn't you tell me all this then?"

"Because I did what I do best, running away." Her hands finally stilled, clasped in front of her. "And I didn't want you trying to talk me out of leaving."

"I wouldn't do that," he said, disgusted that she thought so little of him despite her heartfelt confession. "For someone you think is better than you, you sure don't know me at all."

Her head cocked to the side. "I'm confused."

She wasn't the only one.

"I'm a freelancer. I move around the world for work. It's what I do." He crossed the room to Chantal's desk and spun the small globe perched beside her PC. "I could've accepted more jobs in London. We could've tried long distance." He pinned her with an accusatory glare that he hoped encapsulated the antagonism reverberating through his body. "But you gave up on us."

Her mouth opened. Closed. Before she wrapped her arms around her middle. "You live in a small town. You love it there. It's your home. For me, being stuck in a small town is my biggest nightmare. I ran away from that life because it breeds resentment and boredom in a relationship."

She laughed, a bitter, hysterical sound devoid of amusement. "My parents were desperately unhappy, both having affairs while maintaining the facade of a perfect marriage. It was a joke. And who knows, if I was confined to that kind of life, I might end up a cheater too."

Okay, so there was more to Ashlin than the guilt over the abortion. Man, and he thought he had a lot of emotional fallout from his folks.

"Is there anything else?" He crossed the office and stood in front of her, using all his willpower to keep his arms by his sides and not reach for her. "Because so far you've lied to me about not loving me, used a job in London, an abortion that happened a lifetime ago, small town life, and your parents' bogus marriage as excuses to push me away."

He paused, pretending to think. "And let's not forget that crap about me being too good for you. Because babe? From where I'm standing, we've got it made. We love each other. We're honest with each other. And we're willing to compromise."

He smiled at her gob-smacked expression. "Well, one of us is willing to compromise. Don't you get it? I don't have to live in New Orleans. I chose small town life because I'm a hermit. I shut myself off from everyone emotionally because it was easier that way. But the way you make me feel?"

He took a risk in snagging her hand and pressing it against his heart. "I love you. I'll always love you. And I don't care where my home is, as long as it's with you."

She started crying. Huge, ugly sobs that made her shake and he quickly bundled her into his arms.

He held her: stroked her back, smoothed her hair, whispered how much he loved her and eventually the tears stopped. When she eased back, her eyes resembled pandas', her lipstick had smudged and her skin was blotchy. He'd still never seen anything so beautiful.

"So we're good?" He ran his thumb along her jaw.

Her lower lip wobbled. "Define good."

"We're working in London for the foreseeable future. You love me. And you want to be with me forever."

Her mouth eased into a breathtaking smile. "That's not good. That's fan-freaking-tastic."

She cupped his face, her joy mirroring his. "I love you and I always will," she said, a second before kissing him into oblivion.

When they finally came up for air, Wyatt grinned. "You know we'll need to rent a massive house so my dorky brothers and your gorgeous friends can visit?"

Ashlin smiled. "You think they'll come all the way to London?"

"Hell, Zane and Steele already traveled here from

lia, and Kurt is finally acknowledging he has siblings, so yeah, they'll come."

Ashlin nodded, thoughtful. "Chantal's plastered to Zane these days and something tells me Miranda and Steele may not be far behind."

"Miranda and Steele?" From what he'd seen, they'd be the least likely couple imaginable. His sedate, reserved brother and the fiery, bold brunette? Not a chance in hell. "Care to take a bet on them getting it on?"

Ashlin screwed up her nose. "No bet." Her smile turned crafty. "But I'll bet on something else."

"What?"

"You and me getting it on for a long time to come." Grabbing his hand, she tugged him toward the door, where she flicked the lock. "Starting now..."

BEG (Steele's story) and **BURN (Kurt's story)**
coming soon!

If you enjoyed this book, you'll love WICKED HEAT!

EXCERPT FROM WICKED HEAT

If you enjoyed the Bombshells series, you'll love the HOT ISLAND NIGHTS series, Wicked Heat and Wanton Heat.

Here's an excerpt from **WICKED HEAT.**

Chapter One

Jett Halcott knew lingerie.

Which meant the tall blonde striding through LAX like she had a bug up her ass, leaving a trail of skimpy, provocative satin and lace spilling from her suitcase, was either a hooker or a Victoria's Secret model.

Either would be fine with him.

He could call out to her and put an end to the sniggers from passengers streaming through the chaotic airport.

But where was the fun in that?

Instead, he scooped up every frivolous scrap that tumbled out of her wheeled luggage, like crumbs for a deviant Hansel ready to gobble the gingerbread all in one go.

He wished.

From what he could see, the blonde looked tempting from behind. Long legs. Sexy ass. Shiny, straight hair halfway down her back that swung with every step she took. Fast strides that lengthened the gap between them.

The lingerie shedder was a go-getter or she was about to miss her plane.

He snagged crotchless ivory lace panties, a black bustier, a red corset, and a tempting assortment of satin thongs and sheer bras from the trail she left behind her, mentally dressing her in each and every one.

Hot damn.

He picked up the pace, dodging weary travelers pushing trolleys laden with luggage, eventually catching up with her after they cleared security.

"Excuse me..." He'd planned on making some smart-ass remark when she turned. Instead, he found himself surprisingly speechless as her eyes connected with his.

Pale, light blue, the color of a glacier he'd seen in New Zealand on a school trip once. Pity her haughty expression matched the unusually striking color.

"Is there a problem?" She glanced at his arms, laden with sexy underthings, and her eyes widened. "Whatever you're selling, I'm not interested."

"Pity. I think you'd look great in this." He snagged a sheer crimson lace thong and held it out on the tip of his forefinger. "Red's definitely your color."

To his surprise she blushed, before directing a death glare at him, the kind of stare that could freeze a guy into hypothermia.

"Do I need to call security?"

"I don't know. Do you?" He returned the thong to the

pile in his arms. "Though I'd prefer a one-on-one fashion parade rather than having an audience."

Her lips thinned into an unimpressed line. "I've got a plane to catch."

"Me, too. Which is why I'm done with my good deed for the day and am returning your belongings." Before she could reply he thrust the lingerie at her and she reacted quickly, managing to catch the lot before they tumbled to the floor.

"These aren't mine—"

"That's what they all say." He pointed at the small suitcase propped at her feet. "Your zipper's busted. You've been leaving lingerie all through LAX."

She glanced down at her suitcase and groaned. "I'll kill Zoe."

Just his frigging luck, she had a girlfriend.

She studied the mass of purple, pink, ruby, and black underwear in her arms and wrinkled her nose. "My friend's idea of a joke, packing this stuff for my honeymoon."

Worse luck, she was married.

Her gaze swung back to him. "Do you think you could give me a hand?"

He waited until a booming boarding call over the loudspeaker finished before responding. "Helping you try them on? Absolutely." He grinned, and for a moment the corners of her mouth curved upward in response.

"I meant could you take a look at that zipper and see if it's fixable." She juggled the lingerie in her arms. "Kinda got my hands full."

"It'll cost you," he said, squatting to take a look at her case. Designer. With a very handy name tag hanging off the handle.

Pity Allegra Wilks was married. She was just how he

liked his women. Tall. Cool. Blond. With a kick-ass Californian accent he found incredibly sexy.

"Cost me what?"

He fiddled with the zipper, unsnagged the silk lining caught in its steel teeth, and stood. "A celebratory drink before we catch our respective planes."

"What are we celebrating?" He smirked. "Your wedding."

And the fact that he'd managed not to kill Reeve, his business partner and former best friend, for costing him the one thing that mattered most.

Maybe he'd reserve that pleasure for the prick if he ever surfaced from his hidey-hole in the Caribbean. For now, he had the distinct urge to see how far he could push the delightfully aloof Allegra.

"Wedding?" she parroted, staring at him like he'd lost his mind. "I'm not married."

She looked away as she said it, and he wasn't sure if he'd glimpsed regret, sadness, or embarrassment before she did.

Maybe this was his lucky day after all.

"You said your friend packed for your honeymoon?" He gestured to her overflowing arms, his mood taking a turn for the better.

"Not that it's any of your business, but I didn't have time to repack." She squared her shoulders and looked down her snooty nose. "I'm heading to Palm Bay without the groom. No wedding. No honeymoon. No frigging happy ever after." She gave him a thumbs-up. "South Pacific, here I come, woo-hoo."

He bit back a smile at her sarcasm.

Palm Bay? No way.

He should feel sorry for her. Or the poor schmuck she'd probably ditched before being shackled to a proverbial ball and chain. Instead, his blood fizzed as he tried to contain his elation.

He'd have a good eight hours on the flight to charm her into modeling some of that lingerie when they arrived.

A guy could live in hope. "You left him at the altar?"

"He left me," she said, sounding surprisingly calm for a woman who'd been ditched.

"Dumb bastard," he said, earning another lip quirk for his bluntness.

"Thanks. I think." She tossed the lingerie into the open suitcase at her feet, zipped it, and straightened to her impressive five nine. "And for fixing that."

"Aren't you going to thank me for saving your lingerie?"

She shrugged. "Considering I won't be wearing any of it, I don't care one way or the other."

He tsk-tsked. "Shame."

She didn't want to ask. He could see the silent battle she waged, curiosity with the urge to tell him to piss off.

Thankfully, her curiosity won out. "Shame about what?"

"A gorgeous woman like you should wear sexy stuff all the time." His gaze started at her feet and swept slowly upward, noting her pearly pink nail polish, white capris, turquoise peasant top, and matching pendant hanging from a white-gold choker.

He didn't linger on the parts he wanted to, like the curve of her hip, her trim waist, her C-cup cleavage. Plenty of time for that. When she was wearing nothing but the sexy stuff.

Yeah, he was that confident. He had to be; otherwise he'd go frigging insane, thinking about what he'd lost and what he faced when he returned home.

"And a bullshit artist like you should quit while he's

ahead," she said, her expression telling him she'd liked his compliment regardless.

A feisty one. Would be just the distraction he needed. "How about that drink?"

Her eyes narrowed to slits of ice. "I didn't agree to it."

"Hmm." He tapped his temple, pretending to think. "Yet I fixed your zipper regardless."

"Thanks," she said, grabbing the suitcase handle so hard he wouldn't be surprised if the thing busted again. But he spied a fleeting glimmer in her eyes, a glimpse of regret, almost sadness.

And he could identify with that. The mess he'd left in Sydney haunted him, probably as much as her being dumped before her wedding. Which meant they shared an unexpected connection. Wouldn't hurt to commiserate together. He could do with a little up-close-and-personal consoling from someone like her.

He touched her arm. "Where I come from, it's not polite to blow someone off after they've done you a favor."

It had been a flyaway comment but something unimaginable sparked in her eyes, something akin to excitement when he'd said the word blow.

So the bust-up babe wasn't as cool as she liked to pretend. He could work with that. His cock twitched in agreement.

She rolled her eyes. "Let me guess. You use that Aussie accent to woo women along with spin bull."

"You don't like my accent?"

A faint pink stained her cheeks as she glanced away. "I never said that."

"Is it working?" He took a step closer, invading her personal space. "Are you wooed yet?"

She snorted, but her mouth softened into a semi-smile.

"It'd take a lot more than a great accent and blatant charm to woo me into doing anything with you."

"Anything?" He lowered his voice, *sotto voce*. "And here I was just hoping for a drink."

He deliberately brushed his arm against hers, enjoying her slight flinch. Which meant she felt the spark underlying their exchange as much as he did. "But I'm definitely up for *anything*."

He expected her to bristle. To shut off. To shoot him down with a cutting quip and an aloof glare.

What he didn't expect was the flare of heat in her steady gaze as she eyeballed him, and the tip of her tongue to dart out and moisten her bottom lip, an innocuous action that shot straight to his hard-on.

"I really do have a plane to catch—"

"You wouldn't want to leave a guy alone when he's down on his luck, would you?" He sniffed and faked knuckling his eyes. "I could do with a shoulder to cry on and maybe you could, too?"

He threw it out there, taking a chance by appealing to her bruised side. She had to be a tad fragile after being dumped by a dickhead. And considering his flirting was getting him nowhere, it wouldn't hurt to change tack.

Besides, he could do with a little lighthearted repartee and sexy distraction before landing in Palm Bay. The place where his future would be decided.

"What do you say?" He flashed his best smile as a sweetener, encouraged when he glimpsed the corners of her mouth turning up slightly in response.

"Let's start with that drink and see what else you can charm me into," she said, giving the suitcase handle an impatient jiggle as if she couldn't wait.

"Lady, you've got yourself a deal."

They were in for a long flight to Palm Bay and he had more than *charming* her on his mind.

...

While her lingerie savior followed up on a problem with his boarding pass, Allegra entered the bar. She'd kill Zoe for packing that lingerie. She knew it was her best friend's idea of a joke, wanting to spice up Allegra's honeymoon on Palm Bay. Ironic, in twenty-four hours her wedding had been canceled, the honeymoon ditched, but a more compelling reason for heading to Palm Bay had presented itself.

A reason that could make or break her business. She'd had no intention of heading to Palm Bay, despite Flint's insistence that she should enjoy the trip. Her ex-fiancé had good intentions, but the last thing she felt like doing after her aborted wedding was take a week in the sun. Until an hour after they'd broken up, when a giant crap cloud dumped on her and AW Advertising had lost its biggest account.

She'd done everything for one of the largest farms in California, from a national OJ campaign to a statewide billboard spread for its avocados along every highway. Her entire company operated on the profits from the farm mob.

And now it was gone. In less than thirty seconds she'd gone from having a successful yet modest advertising agency to being on the skids.

Which meant she needed to secure a new mega-client. A client like Kaluna Resorts, currently seeking a new ad campaign, and her sole reason for heading to Palm Bay.

Kai Kaluna was legendary in the hotelier business. He bought small, secluded islands and turned them into six-star luxury resorts for those lucky enough to afford it. Lush hotels and villas frequented by rock stars, movie stars, and supermodels that wanted to be pampered in complete privacy. She'd seen full-page ads for his resorts in glossy travel magazines, had admired his concepts, and envied the ad agency responsible for boosting his profile.

AW Advertising had to be that agency. He'd won awards across the globe for his stunning, eco-friendly resorts, and running an advertising campaign for him would be worth millions. Millions she now needed for her business to survive.

If she landed Kaluna, along with several new clients she'd pitched for two weeks ago, her agency would be okay. The smaller clients would provide a much-needed cash injection but it was Kaluna she had to land.

Allegra perched on a barstool, ordered a gin and tonic for her, a beer for the hottie, and wondered what the hell she was doing.

Bad enough her reluctant groom had ditched her and business had taken a massive turn for the worse. But now she'd agreed to have a drink with a stranger, something she never did.

Allegra didn't trust many people. She especially didn't trust a slick charmer with *bad boy* tattooed all over his broad chest. He even wore the requisite bad-boy outfit: thigh-hugging black denim, chest-skimming ebony T-shirt, and cowboy boots.

Though in all fairness it wasn't his fault she had a thing for Alex O'Loughlin and the hottie happened to bear a striking resemblance to the über-sexy Australian actor.

That mussed brown hair, unusual green eyes, and day-old stubble did it for her in a big way. Along with the lean, hard bod, the ripped abs, the firm ass…she squirmed. Throw in the easy-on-the-ears Aussie drawl, and how could she say no?

Besides, this was only one drink before she boarded a plane for a week of stress-filled strategizing to nail the pitch of her life.

Plan A, where she married Hollywood producer Flint Dunbar, gained notoriety for her advertising agency, and marketed some of the biggest films in Tinseltown? Gone.

While she lamented the loss of a professional boost, she was secretly relieved that Flint had called off their wedding. Theirs had been a business merger rather than a great love affair. Hell, she'd known Flint for most of her life, given that her socialite parents moved in influential LA circles and Flint was her dad's best friend. When Flint hinted at needing a wife to boost his profile and cement his position in Hollywood, Allegra had done what she did best. Help.

She'd been a helper her whole life, from tutoring fellow students lagging behind in class to tending wounded birds. From saving tables for the nerds in the cafeteria at high school to filling in at the college newspaper despite hating it. No great surprise why she did it, having no support from her parents whatsoever growing up and having to fend for herself. She valued her independence but seemed determined not to see others feel the same abandonment she had.

In the end, it looked like Flint hadn't wanted her help. And she'd been glad. She'd loved him in her own way, the kind of love for a good, reliable friend who would never let her down. They'd had a nice relationship, comfortable.

Which is why she'd agreed to a drink with the cocky, pushy Aussie.

She liked how he'd flirted: confident and teasing, with a killer sense of humor. She admired his boldness. It made her wish she could be more like him, and for the first time in a long time she'd felt *something*...a spark of attraction, a buzz in her belly, a twinge lower. Damn, it felt good.

She rarely dated before Flint, had spent all her time building up AW Advertising from scratch before their three-year relationship began. Which meant she was thirty and hadn't mastered the art of flirting, let alone felt that buzz too often.

The Aussie made her want to experience both. The waiter deposited their drinks in front of her and she paid, wondering if she should drink fast and make a run for it. All these thoughts of flirting and buzzing were a frivolous waste of time, considering she wouldn't see the hottie again after they had a drink together.

The sound of soft female laughter farther along the bar drew her attention, as she watched a sultry brunette place her hand on a guy's thigh, lean in closer, and whisper something in his ear. Not surprisingly, the guy slid an arm around her waist, hugged her close, and planted a hot, openmouthed kiss on her crimson-glossed lips.

A stab of jealousy speared Allegra as she turned away. She'd love to be that confident in her sexuality, that empowered to make a move and not analyze it to death.

"I'm officially nuts," she muttered under her breath, absentmindedly stirring her G&T with a straw. Where did she think this could go? Fifteen minutes of flirtation before they went their separate ways? Yep, definitely nuts.

"Hope you're practicing to whisper sweet nothings in my ear," he said, his warm breath fanning the tender skin beneath her earlobe and sending an unexpected shiver of longing through her.

Disconcerted by her physical reaction to him, especially since didn't know his name yet, she tilted her chin. "I don't whisper in the ears of strangers," she said, her abruptness making him chuckle.

"Is that your subtle way of asking my name?" He held out his hand. "Jett Halcott. Sydney-sider and proud of it."

"Allegra Wilks." She placed her hand in his and as his warm fingers curled over hers, another zing of electricity zapped her in places that were in serious need of zapping.

"I know." He held her hand a fraction too long— not that she was complaining.

"Know what?"

"Your name." He released her hand. "Saw it on your case."

"I'm surprised you didn't use it to your advantage."

"Didn't need to." He picked up his beer off the bar and raised it in her direction. "You're here, aren't you?"

She chuckled, unable to resist his teasing. There was something infinitely attractive about sharing a drink with a transient stranger, something exciting with a hint of daring. Far removed from her usual life.

"You should do that more often," he said, reaching out to trace her bottom lip with his fingertip. "You're beautiful, but when you smile? Wow."

Uncomfortable with his overt compliments, Allegra sat there and let a guy she'd just met touch her lips with a slow, sensual caress. His fingertip traced her bottom lip in a butterfly-soft sweep that left her breathless.

Their eyes locked as he lowered his hand, and what she saw made her wish she could ditch Palm Bay and travel to Australia.

Blatant lust. Strong. Sexy. Seductive. His eyes deepened to an incredible green that matched a favorite jade pendant she wore often. He wanted her, and in this crazy moment, the feeling was entirely mutual.

He raised his beer to his lips and took a long swig, his heat-filled stare never leaving hers.

Damn, she had no idea what to do in this situation. Make a joke to diffuse the tension? Acknowledge it? Flirt?

She hated feeling out of control, had instigated steps her entire life to avoid it. Yet in a loaded thirty seconds, Jett had made her damp with just one look and made her flounder.

"Is the blatant charm an Aussie thing or is it just you?"

Thankfully, he blinked, and broke the scorching stare that made her want to grab a napkin off the bar and fan herself.

"It's me." He leaned in close. "Time you fessed up."

Yikes. Was her reaction to him that easy to read? "To what?"

His lips almost brushed her ear. "You're battling an incredible urge to drag me into the nearest janitor's closet and ravish me."

She laughed at his outrageousness. "Sorry. I don't do sex in cleaning closets. Too many hazardous chemicals."

"Yeah, those pheromones can be killer."

She loved his quick wit and for the second time in as many minutes, wished she'd met him at a different place, different time.

"Pity." He reverted to a smoldering stare that had her wishing she'd ordered a vodka shot chaser. "Sex in confined spaces can be fun."

"I'll take your word for it." Heat crept into her cheeks and she signaled the waiter for a glass of water. To douse herself with.

"Not the answer I was hoping for," he said, shifting his barstool closer so their thighs brushed. "Would've been better if you'd said, 'Sounds good, Jett, let's go try.'"

She cleared her throat and gratefully accepted the

water from the waiter, drinking it all and wishing she could run the cool beaded exterior across her forehead. "How did we get onto this crazy topic?"

"Started with you wanting to ravish me." He clinked his beer bottle to her empty glass. "Seriously. There's no need to hold back. I can take whatever you want to dish out."

Oh, boy.

She could blame her lightheadedness on the alcohol, but she'd be lying.

Thankfully, he reined in his overpowering masculinity to drain his beer, giving her an unimpeded view of his throat and the tanned skin there. Her fingers itched with the urge to touch...

"Hate to cut this short but..." He glanced at his watch and grimaced. "I have a plane to catch."

Ridiculous regret tempered her uncharacteristic yearning to spend five more minutes in his company. "Me, too."

"Shame, really." He held out his hand to help her off the barstool, and while she didn't need it, she took it anyway. "We could've had some fun together."

For the first time in her life, Allegra couldn't agree more.

Maybe it was the shock of having her groom dump her hours before the wedding, maybe it was years of rigid self-control, maybe it was the simple fact that she'd never experienced the gut-twisting attraction buzzing between her and Jett, but what she was feeling now?

Reckless and impulsive and crazy. Crazy enough to kiss a stranger good-bye.

She stared at his mouth, imagined what it would feel like on hers.

"Whatever you're thinking, I like it," he said, tugging on her hand and pulling her in close.

"This is insane," she said, a second before she kissed him, snatching her hand out of his so she could slide her arms around his waist and grope his butt.

Oh wow...firm...sexy...ass... were the only things that registered as he deepened the kiss, angling her head, his tongue sweeping into her mouth with commanding precision.

She made an embarrassing needy sound in her throat, partway between a gasp and a moan, and he drew her to him, the heat from his body making her meld to him.

The dampness he'd elicited earlier with a look turned into so much more when his hard-on pressed against her. To her utter shock, she was on the verge of coming. With Flint it had taken a good ten minutes of foreplay for her to feel remotely turned on, and even then it wasn't a guarantee of an orgasm. How could this stranger have her desperate to rub against him in the hope of getting off?

Hoots and a wolf whistle filtered through her lust-filled haze and brought her back to reality. She wrenched her mouth from his, pressed her palms against his chest—*whoa, nice pecs*—and pushed. He didn't budge.

"Ignore them, they're just jealous," he said, his voice husky as he stared at her lips. "You pack a helluva bon voyage kiss."

Heat surged to her cheeks, and this time when she pushed against his chest he released her.

She didn't want to discuss the kiss or acknowledge how she yearned to ditch Palm Bay and follow him Down Under.

Damn. Bad analogy, considering she still buzzed *down there* in a big way.

His lips quirked into a wicked smile that made her think of long, hot, sultry nights spent naked and sweaty and entwined. "I'm guessing you don't do long-distance?"

She stared at him in disbelief. "One kiss and you want a relationship?"

"Babe, you misunderstood." He trailed a fingertip along her jaw, lingering just below her mouth, where her lips still tingled. "Long-distance means phone sex."

This time, the heat from her cheeks seeped southward. She'd never done phone sex, yet there was something about Jett that made her want to try.

She could imagine listening to that lazy Aussie drawl murmuring dirty words, telling her how to touch herself while he jerked off...

Damn. Not helping.

"How about it?" He leaned in close to murmur in her ear. "Wouldn't you like to get hot and bothered without an audience next time?"

What she'd like is to get extremely hot and bothered, but with him present, not on the end of some stupid phone. Considering they'd never see each other again, she summoned the bravado to tell him.

"What I'd really like..." She slid her hand around the back of his neck and lowered his head so her lips grazed his ear. "You and me. Naked. Having hot and sweaty, unforgettable, wild, climb-the-walls sex."

"Fuck," he said, turning his head a fraction to claim her lips again.

With her body straining toward him and her panties so damp she'd have to change into one of those mortifyingly skimpy things Zoe had packed, she put every ounce of yearning into the kiss. Not surprised at her sigh of disappointment when they eased apart.

"I have to go," she said, grabbing her suitcase handle and making a run for it before she changed her mind.

As she strode away on wobbly legs without looking back, she wanted him to come after her. She wanted him to take her up on the brazen offer she'd thrown out, knowing full well he couldn't.

She wanted him. Period.

But he didn't come after her and she didn't look back. And for one, insane moment she thought her wishful imagination had conjured up a murmured "see you soon" from the guy who'd made her lose control for the first time in forever.

READ WICKED HEAT NOW!

FREE BOOK AND MORE

SIGN UP TO NICOLA'S NEWSLETTER for a free book!

Read Nicola's newest feel-good romance **DID NOT FINISH**

Or her new gothic **THE RETREAT**

Try the **CARTWRIGHT BROTHERS** duo

FASCINATION

PERFECTION

The **WORKPLACE LIAISONS** duo

THE BOSS

THE CEO

Try the **BASHFUL BRIDES** series

NOT THE MARRYING KIND

NOT THE ROMANTIC KIND

NOT THE DARING KIND

NOT THE DATING KIND

The **CREATIVE IN LOVE** series

THE GRUMPY GUY

THE SHY GUY

THE GOOD GUY

Try the **BOMBSHELLS** series

BEFORE (FREE!)

BRASH

BLUSH

BOLD

BAD

BOMBSHELLS BOXED SET

The **WORLD APART** series

WALKING THE LINE (FREE!)

CROSSING THE LINE

TOWING THE LINE

BLURRING THE LINE

WORLD APART BOXED SET

The **HOT ISLAND NIGHTS** duo

WICKED NIGHTS

WANTON NIGHTS

The **BOLLYWOOD BILLIONAIRES** series

FAKING IT

MAKING IT

The **LOOKING FOR LOVE** series

LUCKY LOVE

CRAZY LOVE

SAPPHIRES ARE A GUY'S BEST FRIEND

THE SECOND CHANCE GUY

Check out Nicola's website for a full list of her books.

And read her other romances as Nikki North.

'MILLIONAIRE IN THE CITY' series.

LUCKY

COCKY

CRAZY

FANCY

FLIRTY

FOLLY

MADLY

Check out the **ESCAPE WITH ME** series.

DATE ME

LOVE ME

DARE ME

TRUST ME

FORGIVE ME

Try the **LAW BREAKER** series
THE DEAL MAKER
THE CONTRACT BREAKER

EXCERPT FROM BOLD

***Have you read BOLD, introducing the sexy Harrison brothers?
Here's a snippet:***

"Marriage is for suckers." Chantal Kramer raised her glass to the hottest guy she'd had the pleasure of drinking with in a long time. A sexy Aussie footballer that had landed in Vegas yesterday and had been a fellow witness at her BFF's wedding today. "An outdated institution for romantic schmucks hell-bent on ruining their lives."

Zane Harrison, a taller, blonder version of Hugh Jackman, tapped his beer bottle against her glass. "I'll drink to that."

"I knew I sensed a kindred spirit when you seemed bored during most of the ceremony." She drained her glass and gestured at Dave, her favorite barman, for a refill. "Can you believe those two had a quickie Vegas wedding?"

Zane shrugged, drawing attention to impressively broad

shoulders. "I only know Reid through Jack, and not very well, so I haven't got a clue why he'd marry Adele so quickly."

"She's pregnant." Though Chantal knew that wasn't the reason her best friend and her cousin had got hitched so quickly.

Adele and Reid were head over heels in nauseating love. The kind of love that transcended boundaries. The kind of love that forgave Adele's escort past. The kind of love that made Reid give up his fast track to the senate to be a family guy with the woman he adored.

And while Chantal openly ridiculed the apparent depth of emotion that caused two sane people to tie the knot, deep down she admitted to a touch of envy.

She may despise marriage and all it entailed, but she'd give all the spangles in her booming business to have a guy look at her the way Reid looked at Adele.

Zane tilted his head, studying her, as if he knew she was bullshitting. "They're old enough not to have Adele's dad come after Reid with a shotgun."

"Yeah, but both of them didn't have happily married parents growing up, so I guess they want their kid to have that."

"Makes sense." Zane nodded, staring at his beer bottle like he expected a genie to pop out. "I should know."

Intrigued that the macho football player she'd only met yesterday would divulge anything beyond the superficial, she glanced around her club, Vegas's premier revue venue Burlesque Bombshells, pretending like she wasn't curious when it was eating her up inside.

In fact, Zane had more than piqued her interest at the airport yesterday when Reid had asked her to play tour guide for the visiting Aussie and she'd wanted to know more ever since. But he'd begged off on her offer for a quickie last night—tour, that is, worse luck—and they'd barely exchanged pleasantries before the wedding today.

She wanted to know more, for the simple fact she hadn't cared enough to talk to a guy in ages, let alone want to do anything else.

"Your parents are divorced?"

The frown she'd spotted during the ceremony returned, doing little to mar his rugged good looks. Tanned, strong jaw, standout cheekbones, and lips that could tempt the most hardened cynic—like her.

"My dad travelled for work a lot. Fell in love with a woman over here. Ditched my mum, my brother and me, started a new family."

His audible bitterness made her want to hug him. "That's why I'm here."

"To punch his lights out?"

One corner of his delectable mouth quirked. "To meet my dad for the first time. And my half brothers."

Something niggled at the back of her mind...the surname Harrison...and then it clicked.

"Kurt Harrison is your half brother?"

"Yeah."

Chantal mouthed 'wow'. Kurt was an NFL superstar. Men envied him, women adored him. A dead ringer for Joe Mangianello, he graced billboards across the country, with endorsements that could keep him in gold boots until he was a hundred.

His eyes narrowed, judging her. "You're a fan?"

"If I say yes, will you leave me drinking here alone?"

His wry grin eradicated the tension bracketing his mouth. "No. Because I'd need to spend the next hour indoctrinating you into the many ways Australian Rules Football is superior to your pansy-arsed game."

She laughed, finding his sense of humor as appealing as the rest of him. "Here's a tip. Don't let that be your opening line with Kurt."

"I'll take that on board." Zane drained the rest of his beer, before placing the empty bottle on the table between them. "Actually, I'm here on the pretext of looking into kicker positions with NFL teams. A few ex-AFL players have been successful over here."

He made it sound like he'd rather dance on stage in a burlesque costume than play NFL.

"AFL?" She was clueless regarding sporting codes overseas but if all Aussie football players looked like Zane, maybe she needed to fast track her education.

"Australian Football League, our national comp."

He didn't smirk at her dumbass question, another thing she liked about him. Since they'd met he hadn't just ogled her boobs and ass, he'd actually spoken to her like she had half a brain, which is more than most of the bozos who frequented her club did.

Increasingly intrigued by this guy, she said, "Why did you say you're using the NFL gig as a pretext?"

"It's the only way I could think of to get my dad's attention." He looked away, but not before she glimpsed a hint of sorrow. "An in."

Her heart gave an annoying twang. When Reid had first bullied her into playing tour guide for Zane, she'd agreed because the guy was eye-poppingly hot and she was in the middle of the longest man drought in history—by choice.

For some reason, Zane had made her re-evaluate that choice. She didn't need to get laid but Zane made her want to. She'd thought bringing him back to Burlesque Bombshells for post-wedding drinks would fuel the spark between them that had ignited at the airport when they'd first met. Which red-blooded male could resist being surrounded by the overt sensuality that her club exuded?

Crimson velvet draped everything, from the windows to the walls. Strategically placed beveled mirrors reflected the lushness back at the patrons: black silk tablecloths and matching covered chairs filled the spacious room, a dazzling chrome bar ran the length of the back wall, and crystal chandeliers dotted the high ceilings.

Prudish people called her pride and joy a strip joint. She didn't care. Because burlesque was beautiful, an art form born in Paris and performed at her venue by the best dancers in Vegas. Bombshells was elegant, classy and incredibly sexy. Just like her, she hoped Zane would think.

But the hot Aussie didn't seem interested in doing the horizontal shimmy with her. And his honest admissions about his family made her feel deeper emotions she didn't want to: pity, and worse, empathy.

If anyone knew about broken families, she did. The resultant fallout had molded her into the woman she was today: resourceful, ambitious, ballsy. A woman who knew what she wanted and made it happen.

Tonight, she wanted Zane. But the pain shimmering in the depths of his gorgeous hazel eyes spoke louder than anything he'd said. The guy was hurting and the last thing he seemed interested in was a fling.

His hand on top of hers made her jump. "Sorry for boring you. Sob stories aren't my usual style."

Trying to ignore the little sparks of electricity shooting up her arm from his simple touch, she smiled. "Weddings will do that every time, turn the most resilient of us into emotional wrecks."

He wrinkled his nose. "You make me sound like a woman."

"Nothing wrong with a guy being in touch with his feminine side." She stared at his large hand covering hers, trying to ignore the old cliché echoing through her head, 'big hands, big feet, big...' "Though if you suddenly don a feather boa or two, I'll start to worry."

His laugh made her belly clench with desire. Spontaneous. Deep. Natural. Like him.

There was something infinitely appealing about Aussie men. They were without artifice. Their bluntness appealed to her low tolerance for BS.

"So you own this place, huh?" He glanced around, his gaze astute. "Impressive."

"I like to think so." She almost preened under his praise. "Started as a dancer here, did some clever investing, ended up buying the place."

"Smart and beautiful." He squeezed her hand and damned if her heart didn't twang again.

Not good. If anything twanged it could never be her heart so she did what she always did when emotion threatened to derail her. Switched to seductress.

"You forgot talented," she said, turning her hand over beneath his to run a fingernail from his wrist to his middle finger, then circled his palm in slow, concentric circles.

His sharp intake of breath alerted her to the fact that maybe Zane would be up for more than talking tonight after all.

Emboldened, she slid her hand out from under his to place both forearms on the table and lean forward, well aware of the cleavage on display from the deep V of her emerald satin sheath.

"I like you, Zane Harrison."

"I like you too." The gold specks in his hazel eyes glowed. "And that's why I'm heading back to my hotel now instead of ravaging you all night long."

Heat streaked through her body at the thought of this big, beautiful guy ravaging her any time. "I don't get it."

"Haven't you heard? Anticipation is the best foreplay." He stood, leaned down to brush a too-brief kiss on her lips, before turning his back on her and walking away.

Leaving her frustrated, annoyed and incredibly horny, while her dumb-ass heart applauded.

ZANE STALKED THE STRIP, surrounded by the glitz of luxury hotels, glam casinos and massive malls. Tourists streamed passed him, pausing to gawk at mega fountains or elaborate shows. Limos cruised by, as flashy as the rest of this place.

Usually, he'd be in the thick of it, reveling in the cosmopolitan atmosphere. Not tonight.

He had too much to mull. Starting with the ridiculous idea he had of reuniting with his dad and ending with the way he'd stuffed up with Chantal.

He had no idea what had possessed him to unburden like that, to dump his pathetic story on her. One minute they'd been flirting at Reid and Adele's wedding, the next he was blurting his sorry family tale.

As for her overt come-on…it had been sheer, torturous hell walking away from the stacked, tall, leggy blonde when she'd wanted him as much as he wanted her.

All that foreplay anticipation bullshit had been just that: bullshit. Because he knew the real reason he'd run when he could've been buried deep inside her right now.

He wanted to break the habits of his past.

"Fuck," he muttered, swiftly sidestepping a pair of rambunctious kids tearing after their parents, as he wondered if he'd done the right thing.

Trying to make amends for the past by being a better person might be nice in theory, but the ache in his balls insisted he was an idiot for passing up a night of raunchy fun.

For that's exactly what spending time naked with Chantal would entail: wicked, wanton, pure fun.

He knew her type. Strong, confident, secure in her own skin and not afraid to articulate what she wanted. The kind of woman he was attracted to, because she knew the score and wouldn't be left broken-hearted when he moved on.

The kind of woman he wished his mum could've been. Sadly, when Christopher Harrison left Patricia, his mum had fallen apart and never recovered.

She'd lied to them, telling his older brother Steele and him that their dad was dead. He still resented her for it. For hiding the truth until three years ago, when she'd told them everything that night in hospital when she'd died of heart failure. Broken heart, more like it, considering she'd never remarried and was emotionally detached from everyone including her sons.

Zane knew he should hate his father. The minute he'd discovered Christopher Harrison's existence he'd Googled him, stunned to discover how wealthy Christopher was, how his sporting goods company was one of the biggest in America, how he'd fathered two more sons with his ex-model wife.

Christopher had ditched his Aussie family to start a new one in America and hadn't looked back. Hadn't reached out to his Aussie sons. Hadn't given a flying fuck when Patricia died.

It had taken Zane a year to work off his resentment and he'd done it the only way he knew how: by killing the opposition every time he stepped onto a footy field.

He'd taken his team to a premiership that year, had won every accolade possible, from his team's best and fairest, to the Norm Smith and Brownlow medals. He'd been on fire, kicking over a hundred goals that year, a guy no center-half-back could stop. Invincible, on and off the field. The women couldn't get enough of him. He'd lost count of the number he'd slept with. Partied with. Crossed the line with.

But it had taken its toll, that year of trying to burn the bitterness out of him, of trying to ignore the hurt, of forgetting.

His game had turned to shit the last two years and when his tibia snapped in a tackle gone wrong, he'd called it quits. He'd taken it as a sign to grow the fuck up and had spent countless hours in rehab thinking: about his future, about his past, about reconciling the two.

He hoped meeting his dad would go some way to doing just that.

When he reached Circus Circus, he stopped, turned and headed back to the MGM where he was staying, wishing he hadn't reneged on Chantal's offer.

He may have vowed to clean up his act, but that didn't mean he couldn't have a little fun while he did it. Besides, in walking away from her tonight he'd proved he *was* different to the shallow bastard of three years ago, when he would've bedded her without a second thought.

He didn't want his sex life to be like that anymore. A quickie act, empty, meaningless. He wanted...more. Not a relationship, per se, but a connection that meant something beyond satisfying an urge, a way to let off steam or burn off frustration.

Chantal had offered to show him around. He'd be seeing her again. Maybe next time he wouldn't be such a sap.

Maybe next time he'd explore the possibility of *more*.

~

READ BOLD NOW!

EXCERPT FROM BRASH

Curious to see how Bombshells started? Here's a snippet from BRASH:

CHAPTER ONE

Burlesque Bombshell Basics

Sexy on the inside translates to sexy on the outside.

Jess Harper was the first to admit, sex made her uncomfortable.

Not the act itself, despite the lackluster efforts by her ex, but the paraphernalia that surrounded her every time she stepped into Burlesque Bombshell, her cousin's Vegas dance venue.

The nipple tassels and diamante thongs and shiny poles made her feel inadequate. Like all that overt sexiness screamed she was a failure in the boudoir. She wasn't. It was the dorks she allowed in there that needed lessons: Getting It On 101.

She pushed through a phalanx of fuchsia feather fans and slipped into the main dressing room, only to be confronted by nudity.

"Jeez, put some clothes on," she said, unable to resist brushing against the vermillion velvet walls as she entered. The plushness of this room never failed to bring out her inner vixen.

"Don't like the view? You know where the door is." Zazz, Burlesque Bombshell's premier dancer, leaned closer to the gilt edged, beveled mirror and puckered up, before slicking vivid crimson across her lips.

"Not a problem. But then who'd plan your gargantuan wedding, huh?" Jess picked up an armful of feather boas and draped them over a mannequin before slouching on a plush peacock blue suede daybed. "Wedding of the century, babe. Your quote, not mine."

"Whatever." Zazz batted her eyelash extensions and pouted. "Table arrangements finalized?"

"Yep. Ruby linen tablecloths. Matching chairs tied with black bows. Elongated glass vases filled with ebony crystals and long feathers. Silverware. Black candles. And bling name holders—"

"Whoa. Detail overload." Zazz held up her hands. "As long as it matches the pics of that swank London Goth wedding you showed me in a bridal mag, I'm happy."

"Easy to please." Jess used her hand as a fake notebook and jotted with an imaginary pen. "Not."

"You're snooty because I haven't told you the venue yet." Zazz sniggered. "Trust me, you're going to love it."

Jess didn't have to love it. In fact, she couldn't give a flying fig if the venue had rope swings hanging from the roof and chains from the chandeliers. The faster she was done doing this favor for her mom, who'd coerced her into planning this wedding from her sickbed, the faster she could figure out what she'd do with the rest of her life.

One thing Jess knew for sure; it wouldn't be helping Pam, her flamboyant mom, plan any more crazy weddings.

"And wait 'til you hear about the food." Zazz shrugged into an emerald satin kimono embroidered with topaz crystals. "Michelin starred. Exotic. To die for."

"Good. Faster I know about the cake, faster I can get onto the cake table decorations."

Zazz cinched the sash at her waist, accentuating her knockout hourglass figure. "The chef should be here shortly so you can sit down together and go over boring deets like which canapés go with which wines."

"Goody." Jess clapped her hands in fake excitement. Last thing she felt like doing today was collaborating with some temperamental, egotistical chef. Visiting her mom first thing had been bad enough. "Getting back to the venue. You know I can't finalize everything 'til I see the room, get a feel for the layout—"

"Relax. We're flying you and the chef out to the island end of the week."

"Island?" Jess's jaded soul couldn't help but perk up at the idea of a free trip to some exotic island. "Where?"

"Prince Island."

"Never heard of it." Not that Jess cared. Any place with island in the title? She was there with flip-flops on.

Zazz smirked. "That's because my darling fiancé owns the island. Six star resort and private villas. Totally exclusive. Invitation only."

Jess clutched her heart in mock shock. "Serious?"

Zazz laughed. "Yeah, who would've thought Dorian would be a romantic?"

Nothing the doting groom did would surprise Jess.

Dorian Gibbs owned most of Nevada and ruled Vegas but held his coveted bachelorhood as the biggest prize. Until he'd attended a Bombshell soiree, taken one glimpse at Zazz and fallen head over heels.

Jess didn't believe in clichés but there was something undeniably electric when Dorian and Zazz were in the same room. Pity the odd lightning bolt or two couldn't strike her. She could do with a good jumpstart. Her love life was on par with her career—down the toilet.

"Dorian would gift you the world on a silver platter if he could."

"I'm worth it." Zazz wriggled her fingers into a white satin glove and rolled it up to her elbow, smoothing it before repeating the elegant action on the other arm. "You are too, hun, and you'd know it if you'd ever let me fix you up with one of his friends."

"I prefer my guy to be in the same decade."

"Bitch." Zazz laughed. "Trust me, there's something to be said for an older man." She shimmied her hips, complete with a few crude pelvic thrusts. "They have the moves and know how to use them."

Jess winced. "If that's an indication of Dorian's moves, you can keep them."

"And relish them twice a day." Zazz propped on the end of her dresser and folded her arms. "Seriously, when's the last time you had a date?"

Jess opened her mouth to respond and Zazz rushed on, "One that didn't involve battery operated apparatus."

"I get out."

Zazz harrumphed. "Taking your mom to rehab doesn't count."

"She needs my help."

"She's had a stroke and is taking full advantage of the fact to have you at her beck and call." Zazz shook her head. "Don't get me wrong, I appreciate you stepping in to take over as my wedding planner. But Pam's milking this for all she's worth."

Didn't Jess know it. Sure, she felt sorry for her vibrant mom suffering a stroke that rendered her left side immobilized. And she didn't begrudge helping her. What she couldn't stand was the constant interference in her life when she'd escaped Pam's smothering years earlier.

They may live in Craye Canyon, an hour out of Vegas, but that's where the similarities between her life and her mom's ended.

Pam went through boyfriends like coffee filters. She pranced around town in mini skirts and tube tops, had her hair blow-waved daily and cleaned out the town's cosmetic supply on a regular basis. She planned weddings with panache and style, at odds with her loud, brash self.

Little wonder Jess had chosen an occupation far removed from her mom's flamboyance. Town librarian was staid, unassuming and quiet. It suited Jess just fine. Until she'd heard rumors the local council considered Craye Canyon Library a dead loss and would downsize soon, so she saved them the trouble and quit, leaving her jobless and directionless.

In a way, planning Zazz's wedding had given her breathing space to decide where she went from here. One thing Jess knew, she was tired of her boring life. Sick to death of it. Zazz was right. She needed to shake things up a little.

"You need an island fling." Zazz snapped her fingers, her grin positively evil. "Hot stud. Sun, surf, sex."

Sounded pretty damn perfect. "And here I was,

thinking you were flying me to some island to plan your wedding."

Zazz waved away her concern. "It'll happen, I have full confidence in you."

"The wedding or the sex?"

"Both." Zazz's eyes narrowed as she smirked. "How do you like your eggs in the morning?"

"Huh?"

"The chef?" Zazz fanned her face. "Unbe-freaking-lievable. Sex on legs."

"Yeah, right." Jess rolled her eyes. "Those black and white checkered pants do it for me every time."

Zazz laughed. "Trust me, once you get a look at this guy, those ugly pants won't be staying on for long."

"Chefs aren't my type."

The moment the lie tumbled from Jess's lips, memories long suppressed flashed before her eyes.

An outback holiday in Australia. A cattle station cook. A kiss that defied belief. And a refusal that burned, real bad.

Jack McVeigh graced TV screens the world over these days, a constant reminder of what she'd once wanted and couldn't have. With that bad boy stubble, murky green eyes and lazy smile, no great surprise he'd won the hearts of viewers glued to his gourmet cooking show with the same ease he'd won hers.

Pity the celebrity chef preferred to break hearts along with eggs.

"Trust me, babe. If this chef can't get into your panties, no one will."

Unease rippled down Jess's spine like a premonition. "Who's this mystery guy?"

Zazz glanced at her watch. "You'll see for yourself in five minutes. I asked him to meet us here."

Jess ignored the persistent tingle that maybe, just maybe, Zazz's chef could be Jack.

Impossible, considering Jack was based in Sydney and had enough gigs to keep him busy into the next century. Yeah, she Googled him, so what?

Besides, Zazz had said the chef catering the wedding was an old friend of Dorian's so the guy had to be the same vintage.

She didn't know what bothered her more: the sliver of disappointment she wouldn't see Jack face to face after a decade or the inhuman leap of her libido at the thought of a little one-on-one island time with the sexy chef.

"I need to check my final show times with Chantal." Zazz slipped her dainty feet into a pair of marabou feather mules and tightened the sash on her robe. "I'll be back in time for our meeting."

"What's his name—" Jess called out to Zazz's retreating back, wishing she had half the hip wiggle the sassy dancer had.

When Jess walked, men didn't stumble or gawk. She didn't warrant second glances or come-ons. She achieved exactly what she wanted to—anonymity and serenity, two qualities far removed from her boisterous, cringe-worthy mom.

With a sigh, she stood and wandered around the room, her fingertips stroking the satins and silks, savoring the lush fabrics she could never wear in a million years.

Her fingers snagged on a set of gold spangled pasties complete with sparkly-fringed tassels and she picked them up, held them over her nipples, and grimaced.

So not her.

"Hey Jess."

Shock ripped through the carefully constructed poise

Jess had honed to a fine art over the years as her hands fell to her sides.

She'd envisaged her first meeting with Jack over the years. Kinda inevitable, with her brother Reid being his best mate.

In her scenarios, their first meeting after a decade didn't involve nipple pasties. Or a smoother-than-whisky voice that made her palms sweat, her skin prickle and her inner bombshell want to strip on the spot.

"Hey you."

Not quite the scintillating opening gambit she'd imagined. Then again, having this big, bronze Aussie cross the room to stand less than a foot away had thrown her brain into chaos and her body into meltdown.

"Nice tassels."

His fingertip toyed with the nipple tassels hanging limply in her hand and she stiffened.

In the past, she would've responded with a blush. But after what he'd done to her? The way he'd humiliated her? Not a chance in hell she'd give him the satisfaction of seeing her cave again.

She held them over her breasts, vindicated when those impossibly green eyes widened, the pupils constricting. "Care to see them on?"

He took a step back. "Don't play with fire."

She took a step forward. "Maybe I'm in the mood to get hot?"

He swore. "You and me? Not going to happen."

"So you've said before," she drawled, giving the tassels a twirl for good measure, reveling in his discomfort as he tore his gaze away from her breasts. "But a decade is a long time."

"Not frigging long enough," he muttered, casting a desperate glance at the door.

So she ramped up the tension.

"These?" She waved the tassels in his face, deliberately taunting. "Tip of the iceberg in my new wardrobe. You should see me in the purple suspenders and sheer, crotchless—"

"Enough." A low, warning growl she had no intention of obeying. "Is this the way you treated your fiancé? Not surprised he bolted."

Just like that, her bravado faded, replaced by the dogged insecurity that tainted her botched relationship with Max, and fury at Jack for judging her.

"Fuck you." She eyeballed him, willing away the incriminating tears stinging her eyes.

That's when she saw the glimmer of victory in his eyes and knew he'd deliberately insulted her to push her away, like he had ten years earlier.

He turned and headed for the door, but not before she heard his murmured, "Babe, you have no idea how much I wish for that."

READ BRASH NOW!

ABOUT THE AUTHOR

USA TODAY bestselling and multi-award winning author Nicola Marsh writes page-turning fiction to keep you up all night.
She's published 80 books and sold 8 million copies worldwide.
She currently writes contemporary romance and domestic suspense.
She's also a Waldenbooks, Bookscan, Amazon, iBooks and Barnes & Noble bestseller, a RBY (Romantic Book of the Year) and National Readers' Choice Award winner, and a multi-finalist for a number of awards including the Romantic Times Reviewers' Choice Award, HOLT Medallion, Booksellers' Best, Golden Quill, Laurel Wreath, and More than Magic.
A physiotherapist for thirteen years, she now adores writing full time, raising her two dashing young heroes, sharing fine food with family and friends, and her favorite, curling up with a good book!